AN OPERATIVE'S LAST STAND

Juno Rushdan

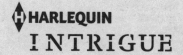

HARLEQUIN
INTRIGUE

This is for Team JIKA. You made this series possible.

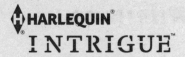

Recycling programs
for this product may
not exist in your area.

ISBN-13: 978-1-335-48940-1

An Operative's Last Stand

Copyright © 2022 by Juno Rushdan

All rights reserved. No part of this book may be used or reproduced in
any manner whatsoever without written permission except in the case of
brief quotations embodied in critical articles and reviews.

This is a work of fiction. Names, characters, places and incidents
are either the product of the author's imagination or are used fictitiously.
Any resemblance to actual persons, living or dead, businesses,
companies, events or locales is entirely coincidental.

This edition published by arrangement with Harlequin Books S.A.

For questions and comments about the quality of this book,
please contact us at CustomerService@Harlequin.com.

Harlequin Enterprises ULC
22 Adelaide St. West, 41st Floor
Toronto, Ontario M5H 4E3, Canada
www.Harlequin.com

Printed in U.S.A.

Juno Rushdan is the award-winning author of steamy, action-packed romantic thrillers that keep readers on the edge of their seats. She writes about kick-ass heroes and strong heroines fighting for their lives as well as their happily-ever-afters. As a veteran air force intelligence officer, she uses her background supporting Special Forces to craft realistic stories that make readers sweat and swoon. Juno currently lives in the DC area with her patient husband, two rambunctious kids and a spoiled rescue dog. To receive a free book from Juno, sign up for her newsletter at junorushdan.com/mailing-list. Also be sure to follow Juno on BookBub for the latest on sales at bit.ly/bookbubjuno.

Books by Juno Rushdan

Harlequin Intrigue

Fugitive Heroes: Topaz Unit

Rogue Christmas Operation
Alaskan Christmas Escape
Disavowed in Wyoming
An Operative's Last Stand

A Hard Core Justice Thriller

Hostile Pursuit
Witness Security Breach
High-Priority Asset
Innocent Hostage
Unsuspecting Target

Tracing a Kidnapper

Visit the Author Profile page at Harlequin.com.

CAST OF CHARACTERS

Hunter Wright—The former Topaz Unit leader has gone rogue and is out for justice. He regards the members of his team as family. He'll do whatever is necessary to keep them safe and clear their names.

Kelly Russell—CIA deputy director of operations. Believing Hunter and his people are traitors, she'll stop at nothing to eliminate them. But she's in a profession of secrets and lies, and the truth behind a national conspiracy could cost her her life.

Zee Hanley—The hotshot hacker is invaluable to Topaz, and not just for her computer skills. She sees what others on her team have missed and is the only one who can save Hunter from himself when it comes to Kelly.

John Lowry—A retired SEAL and Zee's fiancé.

Gage Graham—Member of Topaz. An expert at blending in.

Hope Fischer—A photojournalist who decided to take a chance with Gage, but she's been keeping a secret from him.

Dean Delgado—His specialty is eliminating targets and thinking outside the box.

Kate Sawyer—On the run with Dean, she is the team's medic.

Prologue

Eighteen months ago

Hunter Wright strolled down the seventh-floor hallway of the Waterfront Hotel alongside Kelly Russell, aka the ice queen. She was his team handler and supervisor, for all intents and purposes. For five years, they'd worked closely, executing some of the CIA's toughest covert assignments to eliminate high-value targets abroad, with him leading his Topaz unit in the field and her managing their intel as well as logistics from Langley.

This was the first time they'd ever been one-on-one. Alone. Outside the Washington, DC, metropolitan area.

A possibility he'd imagined many times, though, if it were up to him, they wouldn't be freezing their keisters off in Boston. This TDY—temporary duty—attending an international industrial technology conference had been a last-minute thing. They had been sent undercover to spy on attendees after the two operatives who had been scheduled to be there got food poisoning from a buffet restaurant, a total fluke.

Kelly had been the first to volunteer. Naturally, there

was no way on God's green earth Hunter was going to miss the weeklong opportunity to work as partners with her while indulging in long dinners and playing tourist.

Now their time had come to an end. This was the last night of the conference. Tomorrow morning they had to catch a nine o'clock flight out of Logan International.

She stopped at the door to her room and slipped her heels off with a sigh, as though she'd been looking forward to that moment all day. His room was right across the hall, but he lingered beside her, taking her in. Even with her hair tucked in a twist, the conservative pantsuit that did nothing to flatter her lithe body and the barest touch of makeup that let her freckles shine, none of it downplayed her stunning beauty.

After a sixteen-hour day, which had started with them both in the gym at 5:00 a.m., she looked worn-out and a little tipsy from one too many drinks at the bar. Not that Kelly was at a disadvantage. She could hold her liquor, stayed sharp and aware, never letting her guard down.

He knew he should just keep his mouth shut—to speak his mind would be playing with fire. Still, he leaned on the door frame and said, "Hey, think you might be interested in a last nightcap, in my room—*or yours*—instead of the bar?"

She looked up at him and smiled, her eyes a deep cobalt blue, dark fire-red hair, her skin pale and creamy, those angular features, her full pink mouth, the effortless sensuality. It all hit him like a gut punch. God, she was breathtaking.

"A drink? No." Amusement rang in her voice, and something inside him sank.

"All right," he said nonchalantly. He forced a smile, swallowing his disappointment, and stepped across the hall. Of course. Some things weren't meant to be. This was for the best anyway. Everything came at a price. To be with Kelly Russell might cost him his soul. "I'll let you get some sleep. It's been a long week, and we've got an early flight."

"Hunter," she said, and he glanced back at her. "Who said anything about sleeping? I *am* interested in the euphemism behind your offer of a nightcap." Another smile, this time flirty, sexy. Full of promise. "And to answer the second part to your question, my room."

Every muscle in his body tightened with need, making it difficult for him to think of anything else, least of all playing it cool.

"We need to establish the rules of engagement first," she said.

All business. Always in control. Even now. For some inexplicable reason, it only added to her allure.

He strolled back across the hall. "I'm listening."

"This has to be a one-night-only situation. It can never happen again."

He reached out and tucked a fiery strand that had escaped her twist behind her ear. Her skin was warm and soft, with a perfect porcelain texture. "My mother always told me, never say never."

"I'm serious, Hunter." She slipped her key card in the slot, unlocked the door and opened it. "One night to assuage our mutual curiosity."

Curiosity. Chemistry. Semantics. "If we enjoy ourselves, why only one night?"

Standing on the threshold, she held the door open with it at her back. "We need to keep things professional in the office. Neither of us can afford to let whatever happens tonight cloud our judgment or impact any hard decisions we might have to make in the future."

If it ever came down to her choosing between him and national security, she didn't want emotion causing her to hesitate or think twice about that choice. She was destined for greatness. One day, she would be the director of the CIA, and she didn't want anything or anyone getting in the way of her climb up the ladder. He understood—it was the same for him. Nothing would ever cloud his judgment professionally, either. Not even one night with the incomparable Kelly Russell.

"Is that it?" He slipped into the doorway in front of her. They stood so close in the narrow space that their bodies almost touched. He was so physically aware of her that he felt as though he were standing in the middle of a magnetic field, electric current flowing between them, with the air snapping and sparks flying.

"One more thing." She took a step closer, and her chest brushed his suit. "What happens TDY, stays TDY. We'll never discuss it."

He didn't need to talk about it to replay it in his head. "Agreed."

Grabbing his tie, she pulled him into her room and tossed her shoes.

Desire coiled and tightened in his gut. He'd never

been attracted to weak, helpless women who needed protecting. There was nothing weak about Kelly.

She was as fierce and deadly as a switchblade.

The door slammed closed behind them. There was a sweet, faintly spicy scent in the air that overrode the generic flatness prevalent in hotel rooms. His blood stirred—from the proximity to her, from anticipation, from the sheer reaction to the feminine smell, universal in some ways, exclusive to her in others.

"I do have a condition of my own," he said.

As she undid his tie with a gleam in her eyes, he slipped his hands into her hair, something he'd longed to do, and plucked out the pins, throwing them one by one to the floor.

She raised a perfectly groomed eyebrow. "Which is?"

"It's more about clarifying parameters rather than a condition per se." He found the last pin in her hair, and the sophisticated twist tumbled down her back. The long, silky strands flowed in loose waves around her shoulders. "The *night* doesn't end until the sun is up."

Her mouth quirked in a sinfully sexy grin. "I can live with those terms."

He fisted a hand in her hair and pulled her luscious body against his, aching to taste every inch of her.

There were a hundred reasons, all of them good, why he shouldn't have Kelly in his arms, why he shouldn't want this one night with her more than he wanted his next breath, but in that instant, none of them mattered… even though the price for this night might be higher than he could possibly imagine.

THE NEXT MORNING, in the light of day, Kelly pressed her forehead to the cool bathroom door, shriveling on the inside from regrets. Great, big, screaming regrets.

Not because the night with Hunter hadn't been off-the-charts amazing. On the contrary. It had been unbelievable. Better than any fantasy.

But what had she been thinking? To be so weak as to give in to a physical urge.

A conflict of interest of this magnitude could jeopardize her career and everything she'd worked so hard to achieve.

Although she had told him they'd never speak of this—and she wouldn't with him—at the first opportunity, she was reporting this *incident* to Human Resources. She could not afford to have this come out during a counterintelligence polygraph.

That was how operatives were compromised. Blackmailed.

What would happen if the unfortunate day ever came when they were on opposing sides instead of the same team?

Sometimes the unthinkable happened, interpersonal dynamics thrown into a tailspin due to politics, ambition, greed. One thing trumped all others to her—national security.

Cracking the bathroom door open, Kelly put her stealth skills to good use. She slipped into the main room, fully dressed, with her packed carry-on and shoes in her hand.

Sunlight peeked through the curtains, falling on Hunter's naked body in her bed, with only his lower half covered. She watched him sleeping for a moment and memorized the sight of him like this. Smooth skin marred by scars. Every ridge and valley of ripped muscle in his chest and abdomen. Those strong arms that had held her close.

She had wanted Hunter with a blind, ferocious need, a craving she couldn't suppress no matter how hard she'd tried. And for hours she'd fed that particular hunger until they'd both been sated and too exhausted to move.

A pang cut through her, but she vowed, *never again*.

This was lust, nothing more. Certainly not some other four-letter word.

With a deep breath, she steeled herself.

He stirred, his head rolling to the side, blond hair mussed, his hand touching the empty space beside him. His bright blue eyes opened, his gaze finding the clock before locking on hers. A delicious smile spread across his devastatingly handsome face, and her chest tightened.

"Why are you dressed?" His voice was husky, with a gravelly rasp that caressed her senses, making her thighs tingle. "We've got three hours before our flight. Come here, Red."

That was the first time he'd called her the nickname, and it had her belly turning to mush.

With a lazy grin on his face, he reached out for her.

She wanted nothing more than to take his hand and climb back into bed with him. To stay there all day, for another night at least. To forget the outside world existed.

But there was far too much at stake.

"The sun is up, Hunter. The night is over. It's time to go home." Her tone was stone-cold, her gaze unflinching, her expression serious. His smile fell. "I plan to report this indiscretion to HR." She owed it to him to give him a heads-up. "I highly recommend you do likewise. Since this is a onetime thing, I don't think I'll be pulled as your team handler."

Planting a forearm on the bed, he lifted up with a bewildered look, but she pressed on, forcing herself to stare into those crystal-blue eyes and ignore the wild flutter in her chest. "A rideshare will be here in fifteen minutes to take us to the airport." She'd ordered one in the bathroom along with changing her flight to one an hour earlier to spare them the awkwardness of sitting together. Maybe it was a coward's move, but she'd told herself it was a smart one. "If you're not in the lobby by the time it arrives, I'm leaving without you."

Turning from him without giving him a chance to respond, she wheeled her carry-on to the door and stepped into the hall. With the click of the lock behind her, something splintered in her chest, a chilling emptiness settling behind her breastbone. The sensation didn't slow her as she hurried for the elevator, afraid she might be tempted to go back into that room, crawl into bed and climb on top of him.

She was almost running down the hall…escaping. From him.

Chapter One

Never in a million years had Hunter Wright expected to find himself in this position—disavowed, falsely accused of treason, on the run. And now, taking up arms against the CIA, an organization he'd served for more than half his life, had sacrificed and bled for.

All because of the machinations of one woman.

It was the ultimate betrayal.

He wanted to be immune to the raw emotions bubbling inside him, but he wasn't. If only he knew why she had set them up. Getting an answer was a priority, but not the highest at the moment. Notwithstanding an explanation, Hunter was determined to clear his name along with the rest of his Topaz unit.

First, they had to survive the night.

Clenching his jaw so hard that his teeth ground together, he settled into a prone position in the hunting stand nestled between two palm trees with the sniper rifle in his hands. The spot was protected from thermal imaging with a multilayer combination of Mylar foil, which was impervious to infrared radiation and reflected heat, synthetic microfiber spray-painted to match the environment, and he'd covered it with a final layer of nylon camo netting that would take on the ambient temperature. He'd made the perch to blend seamlessly into the landscape.

Two others from his rogue team, Gage Graham and Dean Delgado, were concealed in a similar manner, each with a different vantage point. Ready to bring shock and awe to those coming. Mercenaries—scumbags, not loyal operatives, who had no reservations about committing atrocities—hired to do the CIA's dirty work.

Her dirty work.

But Topaz was prepared, primed for war and wouldn't go down without a fight.

Zenobia "Zee" Hanley, the fourth member, was on the mainland. She and her fiancé were conducting surveillance with their daughter in tow. Gage's and Dean's significant others, both civilians, were no doubt fretting as they stayed at a safe distance from where the action was about to take place.

This was the beginning of the end. Waiting for the enemy to come and lay waste to the island that Topaz— *his family*—had forged into a home wasn't the hardest part for Hunter. What got to him, deep down under his skin, was thinking about the cause of this gross injustice…*her.*

The thought made his gut burn.

"Incoming," Gage said in his ear over comms. "Five hundred yards out."

They'd be here soon. Using inflatable boats with a quiet engine. His guess was electric power propulsion. The strike team would stop more than two hundred yards away, before they could be heard. Then they'd swim the rest of the way.

"How many?" Hunter asked.

"Three boats. Twenty-four men."

Swearing to himself, Hunter gritted his teeth. In his gut, he always knew it would be more than a baker's dozen. *Still.*

"Twenty-six," Dean corrected. "You missed two. They're hard to see this far out, cloaked in the shadows."

"Twenty-four, twenty-six, it's twenty too many," Gage said.

Dean grunted in agreement. "You have to hand it to her, Kell—"

"Do not speak her name," Hunter warned.

"The ice queen," Dean corrected, using the nickname for the woman who was always poised, in control and cold-blooded to the core, "made sure to send plenty of reinforcements."

That she had. "She's excellent at tying up loose ends." Determined, too.

He'd stopped thinking her name a week ago. After he'd learned *she* had been promoted in the wake of Topaz's infamy. Fast-tracked from team handler to deputy director of operations, no less. There was only one way in the world that could've been possible.

She'd set them up and sold them out.

"I'm sorry." Dean's voice was thick with remorse. "It's my fault they found us."

It was *and* it wasn't. The ice queen had spearheaded an operation targeting Dean, who had been in hiding in Wyoming. Rather than kill him, they tracked him and his girlfriend here to this island off the coast of Venezuela, unbeknownst to either. The two of them had led the CIA straight to them, where every other member of Topaz had found short-lived sanctuary.

"No time for a pity party. We've got work to do," Hunter said, needing his team to focus on the monumental task at hand. Not dwelling on mistakes that they couldn't undo. They had to fight as one with singular resolve. There wasn't room for anything else. "I need you both razor-sharp. Once those men have boots on the beach, we have to be ready to push hard and fast. Got it?"

"Roger," Dean and Gage said in unison.

The night was calm and quiet as expected at 3:00 a.m.— the perfect time to launch an assault. A chilly breeze swept over Hunter. To a small degree it was soothing, though he doubted anything would cool his rage other than making her pay for every dirty rotten deed that had caused his team to be branded traitors and marked for death.

KELLY RUSSELL, THE CIA deputy director of operations, stood at the head of the conference table in the vault of the Caracas station. Consular services of the US Embassy in Venezuela had been suspended for quite some time, and diplomatic personnel had been withdrawn years ago. In light of the significance of this covert operation and her need to have boots on the ground as close to the action to get it done right, she was given special dispensation to monitor it from here. She had arrived with the SAC—Special Activities Center—chief, Andrew Clark, and a small contingent of marines to open this section of the embassy and provide security.

Her boss, CIA director Wayne Price, had warned her about going to Venezuela. *Obsession by its nature precludes equilibrium*, he'd said to her. She was known for her steadiness, her ruthlessly cool approach to everything. Except in this.

She wouldn't have stability in her career, her life, even in her thoughts, not until this was finished and Team Topaz was eliminated.

Kelly stared at the high-definition screen that dominated the far wall, watching the live footage from the Predator drone hovering above the target location.

Operation Cujo was in full swing. A fitting name considering Topaz had once been her most envied team, idolized and lauded. She'd even made the disastrous mistake of caring about them. More for one in particular than the rest. Then they turned on the CIA, betrayed her trust and made a mockery of everything she stood for and believed in when the Topaz unit accepted millions to assassinate an Afghan official, an ally to the United States.

Now, like the pack of rabid dogs they had become, they were about to be put down permanently.

"Coffee?" Andrew asked, shoving a hot brewed cup in her face. The man had the aggressive, animalistic tenacity of the weasel he resembled. Alert, dark beady eyes, sharp features and dishwater-brown hair. Always so eager. So bold.

His wool suit was rumpled, the same one he'd worn on the long, private flight, suitable for the mid-March temperature of the Northeast. Unlike hers, which was fresh and lightweight, and more appropriate for the change in climate. The journey seemed to age him, making him look fifty instead of forty. He'd skipped shaving, so he had scruffy stubble that looked coarse enough to sand wood. At least he'd run a comb through his wiry tuft of hair.

She waved him off. "No. Thanks."

After downing two espressos in her hotel room at zero dark thirty and with her adrenaline pumping full throttle, the last thing she needed was more caffeine. Besides, she'd never accept one from Andrew. It might be poisoned.

"You seem…" Andrew said, studying her. "On edge."

Of course she was. This was the most important op of both their lives.

A year ago, while Andrew had been in charge of all covert operations as the SAC chief, she'd been Topaz's handler when the agency's most revered operatives went rogue. Leaving her to take the heat, to clean up the mess and to stitch back together the tatters of her career thread by thread. The suspicion that had hung over both their heads, the interrogations they'd been subjected to—a living nightmare for months.

But she had clawed her way out of that black hole, only to rise even higher, like a phoenix from the ashes.

Everything hung in the balance with Operation Cujo. The question churning in her head now was: Why wasn't Andrew on edge? Instead of being the picture of reserved poise.

She drew in a deep breath, struggling to find the calm center that had served her so well most of her life.

"We need this to succeed," she said matter-of-factly, hiding the desperation pooling in her belly. "We can't afford to let one of them slip through our fingers. Again."

Topaz had made fools of them all since they went on the run. Constantly evading capture, managing to slip out of every trap they'd set. The only member of Topaz they'd never been able to get a bead on until now was Hunter Wright.

Her gut clenched at the thought of him, but it was that fist-tight squeeze around her heart, despite the anger simmering in her veins, that she despised.

She cursed that man's name and rued the day she'd slept with him.

The CIA's failure, her failure, regarding Topaz was getting ridiculous at this point. Another embarrassment was simply something she would not abide.

Those despicable traitors needed to die before sunrise.

"I never thought I'd ever have to say this to you, much less think it, but," Andrew said, leaning over and lowering his voice so that the two marines in the room couldn't overhear, "pull yourself together."

Kelly snapped her gaze to him, bristling at the proprietary tone he had used. How dare he speak to her like that?

Once he'd been her supervisor, but now he was her subordinate.

"You work for me," she said, her voice soft, but her tone full of grit. "You would do best not to forget that."

The smug look fell from his face as Andrew blanched. Catching himself, he washed emotion from his expression. "I only meant you have a reputation to uphold. You're the ice queen, after all."

She gave him a sidelong glance.

"Come on, you know what they all whisper about you. The fear you instill is part of your mystique. But if you're afraid, then it means the rest of us should be quaking in our boots," he said.

She let herself take the slightest comfort in the compliment. "I'm not afraid." She was terrified. But there was no way she'd ever let anyone see her sweat.

"Topaz has no idea we're coming, thanks to your plan to manipulate Dean Delgado," Andrew said. "We have the element of surprise, the tactical advantage, and I put together the best group of mercs. Zulu team will stop at nothing to get the job done. This op is in the bag."

It was true that Zulu was the best of the best. Most were former Special Forces commandos, but it would only be in the bag once they had four confirmed kills on Hunter, Gage, Zee and Dean. Then she would be able to sleep well at night, knowing her greatest shame and the biggest threat to national security had been neutralized.

"I hope you're right," she said. For both their sakes.

She twisted the large, bulky ring on her right hand. It had been her father's United States Military Academy class ring she'd had adjusted to fit her. Heavy men's casting and embossed with the West Point seal where the stone should have been set. Her father had made it all the way to chairman of the Joint Chiefs of Staff, principal military adviser to the president and the secretary of defense, before a heart attack claimed his life. She couldn't help but wonder if he could see her now, what he might think of her and the mistakes she'd made.

Her godmother, Judith Farren, the first female director of the NSA, had already chided her numerous times for getting too close to Topaz. To Hunter.

The phone rang, and Andrew shot her a glance.

Well aware who was on the other end of the line, she gave Andrew a curt nod. "Put him through on speaker."

Andrew answered the phone as she instructed.

"Director Price, Andrew and I are both here. Do you have a visual?"

"I do," he said from his office at the Langley campus. "This is the closest we've come to eliminating Topaz in almost a year."

Eleven months, two weeks, five days. Not that she was counting.

"I dare say this op might be our best and last chance to finally put an end to this." The tension in Price's voice resonated clearly over the secure line. "Operation Cujo had better go off without a hitch or heads are going to roll."

It wasn't going to be Kelly's. She was many things, but above all, she was a survivor. They should be calling her the phoenix instead of the ice queen. She would rise again and again from the ashes, no matter how many times she got burned.

Andrew cleared his throat. "Yes, sir. Rest assured we have the situation under control. This ends now."

Don't make promises you can't keep.

Then again, the more promises he made, the easier it would be to ensure Andrew's head was the one on the chopping block in the event this went sideways.

The one thing she'd learned a long time ago was to never underestimate the enemy, and Hunter Wright was the last foe the CIA wanted to have. He was a former Delta Force operator. The CIA liked to recruit them, but Hunter was special. His contacts ran deep, his resourcefulness was never-ending and his ability to see three moves ahead made him a formidable adversary. Hunter saw angles and possibility where others saw chaos, danger and a problem not worth tackling.

She glanced at the screen.

The strike team had left the boats and was in the water swimming to the island. Almost thirty battle-hardened warriors against eight—seven, really, since one was an adolescent. They had orders to make every effort to ensure no harm came to her.

No matter what, Kelly didn't want to see the young girl end up as collateral damage. She was ruthless, but she'd never intentionally hurt a child or use one as leverage. There were some lines that should never be crossed.

Authorizing Operation Cujo had been a tough call. A painful one.

Topaz had brought this on themselves, and that innocent child, the second they decided to put their self-interests before their country and commit treason.

The strike team had the numbers and the overwhelming firepower, but Hunter would not "go gentle into that good night," as Dylan Thomas once wrote.

He would rage, taking down as many as he could, until his last breath.

HUNTER SIGHTED THROUGH his scope, past the assortment of palms and other vegetation, but his vantage point didn't give him a clear visual of the sea. His line of sight covered the shoreline and up to the house. Ripples tickled the shore, all was calm, but there was no peace. "Give me an update."

"The boats have stopped," Gage said, blowing out a heavy breath. "After checking their gear, they slipped into the water."

"How far out are they?" Hunter asked.

"About three hundred yards. One guy stayed behind."

That man would keep the boats from drifting. "We have three minutes before they come ashore. Have either of you spotted the Predator?"

For a strike mission of this size to eliminate four critical targets and their known collaborators, there would be a drone deployed so the higher-ups could watch the scene unfold on the ground in real time from the safety and distance and comfort of a situation room.

"I have," Dean said. "Eyes in the sky is within visual range. I can see it pretty clearly thanks to the full moon."

It was the sight of a Predator conducting reconnaissance within the past forty-eight hours that had tipped them off that the CIA was about to make their move. A strike team of this magnitude would never be sent in without first verifying the targets' identities and confirming they were on-site.

The Predator was blind to Hunter and his men. The house was currently empty, though it wouldn't appear as such. Eight heat signatures would be detected inside.

A calm stole over him as he closed his eyes and searched his gear by touch, making sure he could put his hands on any part of it without looking, knowing the other two men would do the same thing.

"Is everything ready?" Hunter asked, opening his eyes.

"Yes," they responded at the same time.

Each man had an objective. The three of them had to be coordinated, calculated, precise in their actions.

"Set your timers," Hunter ordered. "Radio silence from here on out until I give the signal."

The radio went quiet as his men complied. This was the calm before the storm. Within minutes they would be in the thick of the action. There was no room for failure. Anything short of success would not only cost them their lives, but also jeopardize the others on the mainland, who were counting on them.

Movement in the water close to shore had him tightening his grip on the long-range rifle. He was capable of taking down targets a mile out, but tonight he needed to bide his time and draw them into the trap they'd set.

After Hunter had found the GPS tracker the CIA had planted when Dean arrived, he knew it would come to this. An incursion on the island. The only way to save his team and clear their names was to face the onslaught head-on. No more running. No more hiding. No more evasive action.

Now they were playing offense.

Twenty-five men emerged from the water, dressed in tactical dry suits, carrying assault weapons, wearing night-vision goggles. Red laser-sight beams painted the night. All those men were prepared to shed blood and ensure no one on his team survived.

Hunter caressed the trigger of his weapon, tamping down his dangerous emotions. He ached to take them out one by one, but with the first shot fired, Hunter's team would lose the upper hand. Without surprise on their side, things would get far more dangerous. They needed to keep the advantage at all costs if they were going to win this battle.

Chapter Two

Conducting a successful operation required the ability to juggle several balls at once, never dropping a single one, while staying focused on the objective. It took training and talent and the gift of knowing when to listen to one's gut.

"Connect the Predator mission commander to the call," Kelly said to Andrew.

"Hold the line, Director, while I patch them in," Andrew said to Price before dialing.

The two-person Predator crew that consisted of a pilot and a sensor operator, a company-grade officer and senior airman respectively, were sitting in a Conex box out in the desert at Nellis Air Force Base. One or both were probably wired from energy drinks.

"This is First Lieutenant Matthews," a female voice said.

"Kelly Russell, here, as well as the director."

"Yes. We're in position."

When Predator missions were conducted in daylight, following a car or target, they always flew too high to be spotted or heard. At night, though, a false sense of confidence had a tendency to set in.

"What's your altitude, Lieutenant?" Kelly asked.

"We are at a half-nautical-mile standoff at eight thousand feet."

"You're a little close, aren't you?" Two nautical miles at twelve thousand feet would've given Kelly a warm and fuzzy. She didn't expect Hunter to be awake at this hour, but there was no sense in taking unnecessary chances.

This wasn't good.

"We were briefed there was no danger of the target catching sight of us, much less hearing our engines, ma'am," Lieutenant Matthews said.

Kelly stiffened, her pulse spiking. "Briefed by whom?"

"SAC Chief Clark, ma'am."

Andrew pressed his lips together, avoiding eye contact with her for an interminable moment. "It's three o'clock in the morning," he finally said, trying to muster a dismissive tone. "Topaz has lowered their guard thinking they've gotten away with it. They don't have anyone on watch. They're all asleep in their comfy beds."

"We hope," she said, knowing that there were no guarantees.

Andrew's scoffing laughter slithered under her skin. "The Predator's altitude is fine and won't have any impact on the mission."

Every factor, every tiny detail could have an impact on the outcome of an operation. This was only further proof to substantiate why his head should roll and not hers.

Taking a deep breath, she refused to let Andrew distract her. She wasn't going to be sidetracked by someone else's incompetence. So, she let it go. For now.

Andrew watched her a moment before taking a seat at the conference table and facing the monitor.

She turned her full attention to the op in progress on the screen. There was a picture in picture. The larger one was the real-time Predator footage, and the smaller picture that was set off in the upper right corner showed the feed from Zulu Prime's body camera.

Zulu team ascended from the water, weapons at the ready, and swept up the beach, approaching the house.

"Here we go," Kelly said, her gaze glued to the monitor.

Silence filled the room.

Thus far, the sneak attack was going smoothly, as planned, and that's what worried her. The men moved unimpeded. No concealed claymore mines were tripped and detonated. No hidden dangers emerged.

Yet the sinking feeling that something bad was going to happen churned inside her.

"Switch to thermal imaging," Kelly said to the Predator commander.

On the screen, the display changed. Twenty-five men became glowing images as they moved in a single line up the beach.

There were heat signatures in the house. Eight. The same number that had been detected earlier.

Still, warning prickled her skin. She scanned the surrounding area, not only for the telltale orange-red glow of people hiding in wait to launch an ambush, but also for any black holes—a clear indicator that someone was deliberately masking their heat signature.

Though someone shrewd, a seasoned operative like Hunter, would know how to effortlessly disappear without a trace.

Maybe she was being paranoid, looking for a trap where there was none.

She had played out this operation evening after evening in her head, envisioning the outcome, and she needed this victory so badly she could taste it on the tip of her tongue.

"Satisfied with the thermal imaging, Kelly?" the director asked.

Not by a long shot, but what could she say? *I've got a bad feeling this op is going to backfire in our faces.*

To get the director and Andrew to listen, she needed something concrete, not simple conjecture of what she guessed was going on. They already thought she was losing her cool. She couldn't have them thinking she was losing her nerve as well. "Yes, sir."

"Switch it back," the director said, "so I can see what's happening."

The Predator crew toggled back to the first sensor.

Some of the tactical strike team mounted the porch steps swiftly yet methodically while the others maneuvered around to the back of the house. Four climbed up onto the roof of the porch, prepared to go in from the top floor.

The men halted a moment.

"Zulu Thirteen, are you in position?" the voice of Zulu Prime, the team leader, filled the situation room.

They could listen in on the strike team's comms, and their end was muted to them. Kelly would only speak to them if absolutely necessary. It was better to let those mercs focus and do their job.

"In position," another deep, low voice said. "Sweeping our entry point."

Kelly's fingers tingled from unease. Drawing in a calming breath, she rubbed her father's ring for good luck.

THE STRIKE TEAM had swept up the beach headed to the big white house. Hunter's home. The place where they'd held family dinners, gathered to talk and to play games. Where they had hatched this plan and discussed the intricacies and potential complications and strategized various scenarios at length.

This was the one constant that would not vary. Any tactical team sent would go for the main house, the location of the signal, and begin eliminating targets there before expanding their search.

Finger on the trigger, Hunter breathed deep, steady, slow.

Hold.

Hold.

His men would do likewise. The smallest slipup, any premature act, and everything would be ruined. Their one chance at this would be lost. No matter how tempted they might be to leap into action. Their discipline and training would ensure they waited until the enemy was in the kill zone.

Dean had come up with this snare, and Zee's fiancé, a former Navy SEAL, had helped him put the components in place.

The covert operators crept up to the house and surrounded the perimeter. One outside light that Hunter had deliberately left on blinked out into darkness. That meant the power had been cut.

Ten men moved, silent as ghosts, up the steps and onto the porch. The point man raised his fist, giving the signal for them to stop. Then he pressed fingers to his ear. To his Bluetooth comms device. Probably listening and waiting for the others to get into place at the back door of the house. Four men climbed the roof of the porch.

The men huddled at the front entrance pulled out a device and slipped it under the door. A camera. They were checking for trip wires and booby traps.

Smart, but Hunter had anticipated that, and it wouldn't be enough to help those mercenaries.

A minute later, the point man waved two fingers forward, giving the directive to breach.

This was it. Hunter sighted through his scope. "On my mark," he whispered into his comms. "We're going to rain hell down from on high."

THE SITUATION ROOM was quiet enough to hear a pin drop. Tense and watchful, Kelly waited. She clutched the back of the chair she stood behind and dug her manicured nails into the cushy leather. The *ticktock* from a clock on the wall that still worked reverberated through her.

Andrew propped his forearms on the table, clasping his hands almost as if in prayer, and leaned in toward the screen.

Zulu team had cut the power, but surely Hunter had an alarm system with a backup battery. The alarm would go off, screaming like banshees, the second the team breached the house, waking everyone inside. Zulu would have to move fast. That was why they had men positioned on the upper floor.

About a hundred things could go wrong, and there was only one way this would go right. Everything had to work exactly as planned.

"All clear," Zulu Prime said.

"All clear," Thirteen responded.

Zulu Prime gave the signal. The front door was busted in.

An alarm went off, the screeching sound over their comms rubbing her already raw nerves like sandpaper. The team rushed inside, and the Predator lost visual of them.

Quickly, she typed in commands on the keyboard to swap the picture-in-picture screens, giving the team leader's body cam footage the larger display.

Choppy orders from Zulu and curt responses bounced back and forth across the line. The heavy thud of boots pounding across a floor filled her ears as they searched the house. Doors opened and closed as they called out *clear*, notifying the others a room was empty.

"Damn, that isn't good," someone said. "This is Zulu Five. There's no one upstairs."

"What?" Zulu Prime asked, slowing down as he spoke. "We have confirmed heat signatures up there."

"They put SmartDummies in the beds."

Thermal manikins. Human models designed for scientific testing that could be programmed to reach twenty to thirty degrees Fahrenheit over ambient room temperature. They were hard to come by unless you had the right connection.

But if the eight individuals they had surveilled while doing recon weren't in the house, then where were they?

Zulu Prime eased forward into the next room. There was something stacked up on the center of a table with a blinking light.

"What is that?" Andrew asked, peering at the monitor.

Zulu Prime drew closer to the object. "Oh, no." His tone sent chills up Kelly's spine. "Get out! Get out! Retreat!" He whirled around and ran for the hall.

The airwaves cracked like a living thing. A series of loud pops resonated followed by a hissing sound.

"Halothane," someone said.

The men in front of Zulu Prime dropped like puppets with their strings cut. A split second after, Prime fell, too.

Then in the smaller picture window, an explosion ripped through the air behind the house.

What was that? A generator?

She checked the feeds from the other body cameras. The majority of the team was down. Knocked out in one fell swoop.

Hunter must've had canisters of halothane hidden throughout the whole house. The clear, colorless gas had a sweet chloroform-like odor. The amount needed to flood the place would leave those men nauseous and vomiting with chills and severe headaches once they woke up.

Shock seized her every muscle as the undeniable reality hit her. Zulu had walked into a trap set by Hunter. He'd known. Somehow that man had known they were coming, and rather than flee with his tail tucked between his legs, he'd stood his ground and fought.

Andrew hung his head, holding it in his hands.

Kelly put the Predator footage back on the main screen.

The Zulu stragglers who hadn't been incapacitated were racing down the beach, desperate to reach the water. Muzzle flashes erupted on the screen right before three individuals emerged out of nowhere. Lighting up the beach with live rounds and tracer fire were Hunter and two others. Her guess, it was Gage and Dean.

Crafty devils. They were using classic guerrilla warfare tactics to level the battlefield. A show of force to make her think twice. But she would not be so easily deterred.

Even as part of her recognized their elite skills and unwilling pride swelled in her heart, the other part of her loathed them for being the bane of her existence.

To think her father had held Hunter in such high esteem, thought he might make a suitable partner for her if he ever left the CIA and became a contractor. An equal in every way. Provided she dared to open herself to a relationship.

If her dad could see the traitor Hunter had become, one who was besting her, he'd roll over in his grave.

Aghast, she watched the remaining men from Zulu fall one after the other and eventually stop moving.

Suddenly, the beach went dark. Except for the blazing inferno behind the house.

"This can't be happening," Andrew whispered, on the brink of panic. "This *can't* be happening."

But it was happening. To her.

No battle plan survives contact with the enemy. The axiom her father had ingrained in her slid through her head.

"When a plan falls apart and mistaken suppositions come back to bite you, be prepared to sink your teeth into something—or someone," her father had told her.

Shaking her head, Kelly snapped out of her shocked stupor. She whipped out a secure cell phone, a burner, and hit the only number programmed on speed dial. "It's me," she said when it was answered.

"Do I have a green light?" the baritone voice on the other end asked with a hint of twisted amusement. The *thwomp, thwomp, thwomp* of rotator noise played in the background.

"You are cleared hot to go. Topaz doesn't leave that island alive."

She heard the smile in his voice as he said, "Yes, ma'am. It'll be my pleasure."

Kelly disconnected, and nausea bubbled in her stomach. Had she just unleashed a bigger devil than the one she was trying to catch?

Andrew turned to her as if waking from a trance. "Wh-who was that? Who were you talking to?"

"Beta team." Her contingency plan. "I had them keep out of Zulu's sight." And far from Andrew's purview. "They're two minutes from having boots on the island." They were coming in by helicopter and would rappel in.

Beta wasn't led by the best of the best. Their team leader was the worst of the worst, as in bad to the bone. He was an unscrupulous man who had no honor, cared nothing about collateral damage and would go through his own grandmother to get the target if the payday were big enough.

But desperate measures and all.

"Maybe this can be salvaged, after all," the director said. "Good thinking, Kelly."

She wanted to thank him, but that would've been premature. Her Beta team had to get to that island ASAP and finish the mission objective first. In the event the tide didn't turn in her favor, she needed to be prepared.

Kelly beckoned to one of the marines, and once he was close enough, she leaned in. "Prepare to lock up in case we need to make a hasty exit. Then have the vehicles ready and waiting," she said in a hushed tone.

"Yes, ma'am." The marine left the room.

Andrew stood, his mouth agape, his face mottled red, his eyes narrowed, seething. "You…you had a backup team and didn't tell me? How could you keep this from me? I should have been informed."

"I don't answer to you." She cut her gaze to him. "You work for me, not the other way around. Remember?"

Chapter Three

They did it. Their plan had worked, and they'd gotten rid of the private army that had been sent to terminate them.

This was a temporary victory, since the war had yet to be won. Hunter wasn't deluding himself about their situation, but he would gladly take the win.

As they took the slightest moment to catch their breath, he didn't allow himself to relax. He stayed tense, ready for anything. They still had to make the trek to the other side of the island to reach their egress point and get away without the Predator tracking them.

"Hey," Gage said, looking around, "do you hear that?"

"No, what is it?"

Gage tilted his head back and searched the sky.

"There!" Dean pointed. "We have incoming."

Hunter followed the direction Dean had indicated.

A black helicopter was inbound. A tactical stealth model.

The hairs on his arms and the nape of his neck lifted as he experienced a disconcerting sense of déjà vu. In the moonlight and with the open doors, it was easy to make out a secondary strike team with men strapped in as well as riding the external benches, locked and loaded, coming in hot and heavy.

"A damn backup team?" Hunter's rough estimate was ten men in the helicopter. There might be more in that bird. He wouldn't know for certain until they dropped in. But he wasn't sticking around long enough to find out.

The ice queen was gunning for them. That was for sure. She'd had a secondary strike unit waiting in the distance just in case the first failed. If there had been any question in his mind that she was responsible for setting them up, it was now gone.

Without a shadow of a doubt, she wanted Hunter and his people dead.

His fury was a hot fire, and this only stoked the flames to burn hotter.

Hunter tore his gaze from the helicopter. "Those men will be overhead and rappelling down within two minutes."

"I take it we're not sticking around to greet those guys," Dean said.

"Definitely not." Hunter wasn't one to get rattled. Panicking never solved a problem. Every step they needed to take was solid in his mind. "Go to your hidey-holes and grab your thermal imaging shielding. They can't track what they can't see." He glanced at his watch. "You have sixty seconds. Meet me at the rendezvous point. Hustle, hustle!"

They dispersed, taking off in different directions. Hunter bolted through sand and grass to the tree stand.

He climbed the trunk faster than a monkey. Inside the platform, he tore off the DIY shielding from the top and around the sides of the stand. He tossed it over the edge, down thirty-five feet, hoping it didn't break apart on the branches of the trees below, and then he leaped off the platform with his rifle in hand.

Jumping was easy. Anyone could jump. Landing without breaking multiple bones was the trick. He plummeted through fronds, branches whipping at his face and arms. It was all he could do to keep one arm in front, preventing the branches from hitting him in the eye.

The ground rushed up at him. He landed on the balls of his feet and into a tuck and roll unscathed. Luckily, his shielding remained intact.

The Predator wouldn't be able to track them with thermal, but it had other sensors that would still detect their movement. The smoke from the explosion would help cover their trail, but they would not be invisible.

The faster they moved, the higher the odds of them surviving this second-wave attack.

The *thwomp*, *thwomp* from the rotor blades drawing closer pounded in his ears, driving his pulse harder. A crew of former Special Forces turned guns for hire was about to descend on them, and he'd already played his trump card.

Taking out the enemy was no longer the priority. They needed to get off this island. Now.

The helicopter was directly over the beach. Four ropes dropped and dangled from the bird.

Scooping up the thermal shielding and wrapping it

around himself, he hustled toward the rendezvous point before incoming gunfire was bearing down on him and tearing up the foliage around his head.

Hunter was highly trained and had a laundry list of skills, but dodging a bullet wasn't one of them. He sprinted through the thick undergrowth. Fifty yards north and thirty yards west. That's where they were meeting.

As he raced through the small patch of jungle, his pulse throbbed in his head, his heart hammering steady as a metronome despite the danger. Mentally, he kept count of how far he'd traveled and instinctively knew when to turn. He shoved branches out of his way, leaping over a shrub, and pressed on to the other beach.

Bursting through the dense vegetation, Hunter caught sight of Dean, who was waiting and geared up, ready to go. But where was Gage?

Time was of the essence. If they got embroiled in a shoot-out with those commandos, it wouldn't bode well for them. The only way off the island in that event might be in a body bag.

But there was no way he was leaving any of his people. One team, one fight. No man would be left behind on his watch.

Four men attached to the ropes dangling from the helicopter and rappelled down, disappearing on the other side of the trees near the house. Four more prepared to follow.

Come on. Where are you?

"Get going," Hunter said to Dean. "I'll stay behind and wait for him."

Dean shook his head. "We stick together. If that team catches up and things get hairy, you'll need me in a fight."

This was what Hunter loved about his unit. Any of them would sacrifice for the sake of the team, and no one put their own needs first. They'd been together for nearly a decade and operated better than a well-oiled machine.

An extra man with a gun could make a world of difference if it came down to that, but Hunter was going to do everything in his power to ensure it didn't. "Get in the water. Now. That's an order."

Gage sprinted from the tree line, armed and cloaked in his thermal imaging shield.

Good man. Saved Hunter from going back to look for him.

Gage ran up to them breathless. "They're not far behind." He panted. "They'll be on us any minute."

Hunter and Gage dug out the equipment they needed from their packs. They put on fins and slipped diving masks over their faces, the same as Dean had already done.

The thudding of footfalls in the woods headed their way grew louder in tandem with the whoosh of branches.

Staying in motion, not allowing distraction, they shoved their arms through the straps of their oxygen tanks and put the regulators in their mouths.

Each of them grabbed a DPV—diver propulsion vehicle—and ran for the water.

Gunfire kicked up behind them, smacking into bark and spitting into the sand.

Fire bit into his arm, and he felt the hot trickle of blood but paid it no mind. It was a flesh wound, and he'd have to worry about it later.

Once they were deep enough, they dived into the dark water just as a barrage of bullets followed them under. Slugs speared through the current around them.

Holding the small yet powerful DPVs by the handles, they switched them on and zipped off. Gage and Dean both held steadfast, and if either was injured, Hunter saw no sign of it.

The underwater scooters towed them through the sea, allowing them to ride in the slipstream, away to a safe distance. Normally it only had a top speed of nine miles per hour, but their former SEAL, John Lowry, had brought his skills to bear and upgraded the motors to go three times that speed.

The Predator drone wouldn't be able to detect them in the water at their current depth.

Using his GPS, he charted their course and held the line. They were twenty-five miles from the mainland, but they had someone waiting to pick them up in a boat seven miles out at a prearranged location.

A red light in the water came into sight. It hung from the boat that was there to pick them up.

They slowed their speed, and once they were close enough, they cut the engines. Hunter surfaced first and climbed onto the waiting motorboat. He dropped to a knee under the Bimini top, which consisted of a metal frame supporting canvas that was open on the sides, covering a portion of the boat.

Hope Fischer, Gage's girlfriend, and Kate Sawyer, the love of Dean's life, hurried to his side, taking his oxygen tank and other equipment once he'd removed it and setting everything to the side.

"Are you all right?" Hope asked. "Is everyone okay?"

"I believe so."

Kate gave him a quick once-over. She was a veterinarian and for the duration of this mission also their emergency medic. A role she wasn't thrilled about, since she'd reminded them a hundred times about the difference between animals and people, but she was willing to pitch in and help in any way she could.

"Your arm," Kate said, examining his wound.

Hunter put a hand on her shoulder. "It's not serious. It can wait."

Dean climbed up next, followed by Gage. Neither appeared injured.

Relief flooded Kate's face as she went to Dean's side and took his tank.

Hope threw her arms around Gage's neck before he could take the regulator out of his mouth. She pressed herself to him, getting the front of her clothing soaked. "Thank God you're okay."

Drawing back and giving him a chance to catch a breath, she helped him get the tank off and slipped the diving mask from his face. She ran her hands over him, inspecting him, to be sure he hadn't gotten hurt.

"I'm good." Gage put a palm to her cheek, calming her. "We're all fine."

"We were so worried," Hope said. "From here it looked like World War III had broken out on the island. My head started spinning, and horrible scenarios raced through my mind. What if something happened to you? What if I didn't get a chance to see you again? To tell you how much I love you. To tell you that I want to spend the rest of my life with you. Oh, Gage." Tears streamed down her face as she trembled. "I'm pregnant."

"What?" Gage gaped at her.

Everyone else already knew or had guessed. Everyone except Gage.

Hope had been a ball of nerves about telling him. They'd only been a couple for a few months, thrown together by life-or-death circumstances. Their love was new and blossoming under the harshest of conditions. It only added to her anxiety that Gage never spoke about fatherhood as something he wanted.

Their situation was complicated.

It was high time she'd told him, but Hunter hadn't expected it to be like this.

"There were so many times I tried to tell you," Hope said, "but the timing never seemed right, and I thought that if I waited there would be this perfect moment. Only it didn't come, and then I realized I could lose you in all this."

"Honey." Gage wrapped her in a tight embrace. Shock was tattooed on his face.

Dean ran a hand over Kate's hair with love gleaming in his eyes. He gave her a quick kiss and then exchanged a look with Hunter. They both understood Hope was in a fragile place emotionally. One wrong word from Gage could turn her into a ticking bomb when they needed everyone to be solid and focused.

"Are you mad?" Hope pulled back and stared at Gage. "I was so used to receiving a text message and a phone call from my doctor's office when I was due to get my next contraceptive shot. But we came here, leaving our cell phones behind. I didn't think about it, and when I did, it was too late. Because I was late. Are you upset?"

"I'm not mad or upset, just…surprised. It takes two to make a baby, honey. I love you. You're everything to me. Both of you." He put a hand on her stomach, and she sobbed harder, but they were tears of joy.

Crisis averted. Hunter exhaled in relief.

With that settled, he moved to the front of the boat and got behind the wheel. He turned the key, firing up the engine, and moved the handle into the forward position, taking off.

Once they made it to the hotel, they would regroup with the others and go over Zee's intel. Then Hunter would do something no one in the CIA would expect.

He was going home to Virginia to snatch the ice queen from her ivory tower and confront her. Finally find out why she had betrayed them, upending all their lives.

Nothing on earth would stop him.

Or save *her*.

"MA'AM," THE BARITONE voice said over the speaker, "the targets have escaped. The Predator lost them in the water. They could be making their way to any number of port cities along the coast or heading to a different island. Do you want us to search the remainder of the islet to be sure no one else is here besides the other team?"

Hunter was too smart and cared too much about his people to leave any behind on the island. But she wasn't in a position to take chances. "Search the island." It wouldn't take them long. The patch of land was small, and Hunter's people had been the only inhabitants. "If you find anyone, keep them alive for questioning. Then meet me at my hotel. There's a helipad on the roof you can use."

She hadn't determined yet whether they would fly back Stateside with her or stay in Venezuela.

The first team would be able to make their own way home. They still had a man out on the water with their boats.

"Understood, ma'am." The Beta team leader disconnected.

This was an unmitigated disaster. Topaz had been within her grasp, and now they were in the wind and on the run once more. She drew in a slow, steady breath on a count of four and released it in the same four-count manner to keep from busting a blood vessel.

Hunter and his people would leave the country as soon as possible, but while they were still here, this wasn't over. CCTV was prevalent in this country. More so than in the United States. After a major Chinese telecommunications company helped the Venezuelan government construct an advanced citizen surveillance program, there were eyes and ears everywhere.

"Director, will you hold? I need to patch in an analyst," Kelly said.

"Go ahead."

She entered the code that would connect the analyst she had standing by in Langley to the call. "This is Deputy Director Russell."

"Yes, ma'am," Ebony Williams said. She was a veteran analyst who not only kept her composure under pressure but thrived in the high-ops environment.

"I need you to concentrate the full force of our facial recognition program here. I suspect all four targets may be within country. Tap into the Venezuelan big brother program," she said, referring to the robust surveillance infrastructure already established, "and find them."

"I'll do my best."

She needed more than her best. She needed a miracle. "Also, keep an eye out in case they use any of their known aliases." That would be highly unlikely. Considering Hunter had time to procure thermal manikins, his team would surely have impeccable fake credentials. This was a shot in the dark, but one she needed to take. "Let me know the second you find anything."

"Of course."

She disconnected the analyst from the call.

"Kelly, Andrew," the director said, "I want you back on a plane to Virginia. As soon as possible."

Keeping up the pretense that she had this under control and that her nerves weren't screaming, she mustered an even-keeled tone for the director and an unflappable expression for Andrew. "But, sir, they're still here within country. I'm certain of it. Our window to find them before it's too late is small." And shrinking every minute.

"Your Beta team will find them. You can give them instructions from anywhere in the world."

She straightened, rolling her shoulders back, and gave the hem of her suit jacket a little tug down. "Of course."

"Update me with your ETA from the airport," the director said. "As soon as you land, I want to see you both in my office. I don't care what time it is. Am I clear?"

She fiddled with her father's ring. "Crystal, sir." At least it was a good thing she'd had the foresight to prepare to close the embassy, though, given more time she was certain she could make headway in finding the Topaz unit.

The director hung up, leaving a dial tone since she had already cut the Predator crew from the call earlier.

The flight would give her plenty of time to formulate her thoughts and put together an argument that would protect her. An even more pressing concern was finding Hunter and his cohorts. They were in some coastal city or town. Sooner or later, they would expose themselves, make the slightest mistake, and Beta team would have them.

She had to believe that.

"I know what you're thinking," Andrew said through clenched teeth, rising from his chair, fiery daggers shooting from his weasel-like eyes, his tone blistering.

"If you're a mind reader, I'm the tooth fairy." She gathered her things. "I suggest you put what talent you do have to better use than trying to infer what's going through my head, considering I could outthink you with a concussion."

"You're going to try to pin the blame for your fiasco on my head!"

"I plan to do no such thing." Going for Andrew's jugular would be too obvious. No, she would not be reduced to a game of pointing fingers and sniping at one another in the director's office.

To save her career, she needed to get Andrew to dig his own grave.

"If you go after me in front of the director, so help me, I'll get you and make you pay, you lying bit—"

"Language, Andrew," she said, cutting him off in a smooth voice deliberately modulated by her Ivy League education and years of breeding. "We're both professionals capable of proper decorum, even under the most trying of circumstances. Such vulgarity is beneath us. Besides, you wouldn't know how to *get me* if you had step-by-step instructions." She slung the strap of her purse on her shoulder and fixed him with an icy stare that made him recoil. "I never thought I'd ever have to say this to you, much less think it, but pull yourself together."

A trickle of sweat slithered down her back as she grabbed her things and spun on her heel. She hated confrontation. It always made her anxious, jittery to the point her hands often shook, and that was the reason she tended to clench them or fold them in her lap. That didn't mean she hadn't learned how to spar verbally. She could hold her own with the best of them.

Kelly strode out the door, headed for the stairs. The

only reason she dared turn her back on Andrew without fearing he'd literally stab her in it was the marine standing as a silent sentinel in the room with a loaded sidearm holstered on his hip. She'd brought the military contingent to protect her from all hostile forces—including Andrew.

Chapter Four

In the hotel suite in Caracas, Hunter's entire team gathered around him, as well as John, Zee's fiancé, Hope and Kate. The only one missing from their little tribe was Olivia. The eleven-year-old was asleep in one of the connecting bedrooms.

Zee, their hacker extraordinaire, had messed with the city surveillance system along a specified route as well as the hotel security cameras to ensure they wouldn't be detected once out of the water and making their way to the hotel room.

After Hunter finished giving everyone an unfiltered sitrep—situation report—Hope and Kate, the two civilians unaccustomed to this precarious lifestyle, turned to their partners and clung to them. The embraces were poignant and full of gratitude, highlighting just how close they'd come to death. Zee and John, a former SEAL with more than seventeen years under his belt, exchanged a look that was no less sentimental, brimming with such affection that it made something inside Hunter ache.

They all had someone they loved. Someone who

suited them, someone to bolster them through this dark time.

Hunter envied them and was happy for them at the same time. Most of all, it fortified his determination to clear their names so that they could have the futures they deserved. No such thing as happily-ever-after for a man like him, and that was okay, so long as his team, his family, got theirs.

For one night back in Boston, he'd thought he might have found what every other member of his team had—a partner worth fighting for. The makings of a love you would do anything to protect. But he couldn't have been more wrong.

He had been nothing but a one-night stand to satisfy the ice queen's curiosity.

"What's our next move?" Hope asked with an arm around Gage's waist, leaning against him while he had an arm slung over her shoulder, clearly wanting to keep her close as well.

Hunter stretched his bandaged arm, gritting his teeth through the ache. "I'm not exactly sure." He needed an update from Zee first. To analyze all the available information before making a decision. "But it's looking as if we're going Stateside."

"Won't it be more dangerous there?" Kate asked. Dean stood behind her with her head tucked under his chin and his arms wrapped around her in a loving cocoon.

"Yes, it will be." He couldn't sugarcoat the reality of it. "But there's no way around it. The proof we need to clear our names will be back home. Zee, you'll need to initiate the diversion protocol."

With a nod, she went to her laptop, which was already powered up. She hit a few keys and pressed Enter. "It's done."

Zee was a computer genius. Her program would have the CIA looking for them in all the wrong places, giving them an opportunity to get back to Virginia without being apprehended.

He'd start with the ice queen and work his way to the evidence that would prove they had never specifically targeted that Afghan official. Topaz had been set up to believe the official had been working with a terrorist and financing him. At a supposed meeting between the official and the terrorist, Khayr Faraj, Topaz had been instructed to eliminate Faraj. But instead of taking out the next Osama bin Laden, the explosion had killed the Afghan official, who was an ally to the United States, and a tribal leader.

All based on intelligence from their team handler. The ice queen. As if that hadn't been bad enough, their egress plan out of the country had been leaked. They had barely made it out of Afghanistan alive.

They later found out that Faraj had never even been there, and the Afghan official hadn't been corrupt. He and the tribal leader had been innocent men.

None of it made sense, and it was time he got answers.

Before he could make a concrete decision about their next move, he needed solid intel he could rely on, and there was no one he trusted more to provide it than Zee.

"What have you learned?" Hunter asked her.

"Kelly Russell is here. In Caracas."

His heart stuttered, and the room spun a moment. That was a bombshell he hadn't been prepared for. Why had she left the safety of Langley? Did she want to see his dead body with her own two eyes, up close and personal?

"Where?" he finally managed to ask.

Pressing her lips tight together, Zee lowered her head. Dark spiral curls curtained her light brown face. "I think it's best you don't know."

"What!" Kelly was here, in the same city, with boots on the ground, and Zee didn't want to spill the location? What was she thinking?

They'd never get answers without going through Kelly first.

He stormed up to Zee, but John stepped in front of him with a palm raised. John was a big guy, bigger than Hunter. A Special Forces operator who was prepared to kill to keep Zee safe. Not that she was in any danger in this room.

"We know this is important," John said, using a careful tone, "but..."

"But what?" Hunter snapped.

Zee raised her head and met his gaze. "You're too emotional where Kelly is concerned."

Hunter rocked back on his heels. "She set us up—of course I'm emotional. We all are."

"I think it's more than that for you," Zee said. "I think it's been a lot more since you two went TDY to Boston together."

A chill skittered across his skin. How could she possibly know?

Hunter had been so careful. Played it subzero cool when they had gotten back after the way Kelly had thrown up an Arctic wall between them.

Looking around the room at the others, he noticed Gage and Dean exchanging baffled looks.

Well, at least they hadn't known until now.

"Wait a minute." Dean let go of Kate and stepped up to him. "You slept with her? You slept with the ice queen?"

Gage moved away from Hope and joined Dean. "The woman who set us up?"

In his defense, he had slept with her before she'd set them up. "Once," Hunter admitted reluctantly, struggling not to turn away from them in shame. He had to face this.

"In Boston," Zee said, closing the circle around him.

Gage looked at Zee. "How did you know?"

Yeah, how did she?

"When you two got back, you were both…weird. Staring at the other when you shouldn't have been, keeping your distance more than normal. There was tension in the room when you two were together. Sexual tension. And you got snippy, Hunter."

Snippy was never an adjective that should be used to describe him. "No, I was myself."

"You weren't," Zee insisted. "I was going to pull you aside and ask you about it, but then I realized that these two," she said, gesturing to Gage and Dean, "hadn't noticed. So, I figured, maybe I should let sleeping dogs lie."

"Was it only once?" Gage asked with his eyes narrowed.

It had been many times but only during the one night that he'd never wanted to end. Like a fool. "Yes," Hunter said.

Zee shook her head with a reproachful look on her face. "Kelly played you."

"I wasn't played." Hunter bristled, putting his fists on his hips. "I initiated it."

Rolling her eyes, Zee crossed her arms. "She let you initiate it. Probably on the last night of the TDY, right?" When Hunter didn't respond, she said, "I bet she lingered outside her hotel room door after you two had a few drinks down at the bar."

That was true.

"But while you had those drinks, she made physical contact of some kind to let you know subconsciously she'd be receptive to the idea," Zee said. "A hand on your shoulder, perhaps a graze of her fingers across your cheek, leaning into you while she shared something confidential, personal."

Kelly had leaned in, putting her hand on his forearm, which had later brushed his thigh and eventually rested on his knee as she'd talked about her father. Shared with him stories about her dad, a man he'd known and respected. Told Hunter how she wore his ring in remembrance of him.

He'd thought they had connected, bonded, that those intimate gestures had been a natural by-product.

"She was the one who suggested you both go upstairs to your rooms because it was late. Didn't she?"

Thinking back on it, Kelly had made the suggestion. She'd yawned and asked for the check.

"I take it your rooms were conveniently close together," Zee continued as if reading from a seduction playbook. "Either side by side or directly across the hall from each other."

A sickening sensation churned in his gut.

"I bet Kelly could've simply said good-night and gone into her room and that would've been the end of the evening, but she didn't," Zee said. "She lingered in the hall, giving you an opportunity to make a pass at her."

The shoes. Kelly had taken the time to slip off her high heels, and although he'd thought he had been the one stalling, it had been her all along.

Maybe Kelly's motives had been more insidious back then. Perhaps she had slept with him as part of a grander plan to manipulate, use and discard him like trash.

How had he not seen it?

He was a veteran operative, knew what to expect from the enemy.

Kelly had been his blind spot. A supposed ally he'd been attracted to. Not just physically. Yes, she was gorgeous, but she was also brilliant and fierce.

Deadly as a switchblade. He always should've known that she'd cut him some day, and she was now going after his jugular.

"You had sex in her room, didn't you?" Zee said, driving her point home. "On her terms."

Kelly had lured him in and played him. She'd even

had a new box of condoms in the nightstand. He had been so excited, so thrilled to be with her that he'd chalked it up to her wanting him, too.

"Damn it!" Hunter said, hating himself for the outburst.

"See?" Zee gestured at him. "You're too emotional where she's concerned."

"Where is she?" Hunter demanded.

"This would be a mistake," Zee said. "Going after her like this. You need to be calm. In control."

"Where. Is. She."

Still, Zee hesitated.

"If I have to go outside and get myself locked up in a Venezuelan jail to get her in front of me because you won't follow an order, then so be it." He knew how to pick handcuffs, and he didn't need to break out of a jail cell to wrap his hands around Kelly's throat and squeeze the truth from her lips.

"Okay, I'll tell you. But for the record, I think this is a colossal mistake."

"Duly noted. Where?"

"If you're going to go, you can't go alone, agreed?" Zee asked.

If? Nothing short of a nuclear bomb detonating would stop him from going. Zee was looking out for him, trying to protect him from himself, but her concern only served to annoy him. He was a big boy and had experience channeling his rage when necessary so that it worked for him rather against.

"Fine," he conceded with a wave of his hand. Although he was *their* team leader, he'd go with a chaperone.

Before giving him the information, Zee added, "Andrew Clark is also here."

Hunter stifled a groan over the insipid man's presence. Clark could certainly complicate things.

"One more thing, and it's *important*." Zee caught his gaze and hesitated.

More important than the fact Kelly Russell was in Caracas? That got his attention. "What is it?"

"The secondary team that Kelly brought in. I tracked them from the airport. There was no way to get a message to you and warn you they were coming." They'd had tight communication protocols to ensure they hadn't inadvertently tipped their hand about the ambush. "But I know who's leading them."

Hunter knew it wasn't going to be good. They had enough to deal with and didn't need any further complications, but if it was as important as Zee claimed, then Hunter needed to know. "Who is it?"

"Mickey Quinlan."

Hunter's stomach roiled as Dean, who wasn't big on religion, made the sign of the cross over himself.

"Oh, man," Gage groaned. "That dude is a lunatic. Why would Kelly hire him?"

Because she was desperate. It was the only reason.

Quinlan wasn't sane. No sane person enjoyed killing as much as he did, but Quinlan could be bought. For the right price. Topaz couldn't afford to use their personal resources on Quinlan, but supposedly there was two million dollars sitting in offshore accounts that they'd never seen or touched.

Maybe Zee could pilfer those funds and put them to good use.

"Where is she?" Hunter asked. Kelly Russell had ruined his life and the lives of the people who meant the most to him. Those standing in this room, shoulder to shoulder with him.

That sin was unforgivable.

Getting to her here, in a country that had a strained relationship and no formal diplomatic ties with the United States, was better than trying to do it on American soil.

"She has a marine detail escorting her," Zee said, stalling.

Speed bumps. Those marines would slow him down, but they wouldn't stop him from getting to her. Nothing would. "I'll handle them. Please don't make me ask you again."

Zee rattled off the name of the hotel and the room number. "I'll go with you."

"No way." John shook his head as his features tightened in a fearsome expression. "You said yourself he's not thinking straight when it comes to that woman."

Zee turned to her fiancé and clasped his shoulders. "That's why Hunter needs me. Gage and Dean won't know where to draw the line with him. They won't see if he's about to go over the edge. It has to be me. Either I go or Hunter doesn't go."

Hunter gave a dark chuckle that carried zero humor in the sound. He was going.

One way or another.

Chapter Five

Hurrying around her hotel room, Kelly finished packing her carry-on. She hadn't brought much with her and had only taken out what was necessary to freshen up before they went to the embassy.

Her cell phone rang. The burner. She could tell by the ringtone.

She took it from her purse and answered. "Yes." Hoping for good news was too much after the events of the past few hours—still, she did pray for the tiniest lead.

"There was no one else on the island," Quinlan said, which didn't come as a surprise to her. "We're here, in the lobby. Drawing quite the audience."

They were hard to ignore. No doubt the staff and other hotel guests in the lobby were staring at them. "Hang tight. I'll be down momentarily."

She wanted to give him his instructions face-to-face, and there was the fact she was still working out what those orders would be.

"We'll be waiting."

She did one last sweep of the room to be sure she hadn't left anything behind, and then she stepped into the hall, where she had two marines standing by just in case Andrew had decided to stop by her room to finish their little chitchat. Nothing like two buff, armed men to make a guy acting on bad judgment think twice.

Not that she needed them to handle Andrew. Her father had ensured she was able to take care of herself by having her trained in Krav Maga and jiujitsu since she was six years old.

Andrew would've needed the marines to get *her* off *him*, but she wasn't foolish enough to lay a finger on him without witnesses to justify any force she might use. He'd have bruises or worse and then it would be his word against hers, along with his injury report. An HR nightmare.

As she made her way to the elevator, her secure work cell rang. She glanced at the screen. It was a Langley number. The generic 703-482-0000 always came up on incoming calls from headquarters. Without the extension she had no way of knowing exactly who was on the other end.

"This is Russell."

"Yes, ma'am," Ebony Williams said, her voice soft yet firm. "I have a lead."

Thank goodness. "What is it?"

"Aliases for all the members of Topaz pinged. They're fleeing Venezuela. By different modes of transportation. One by train, one by bus, one by boat and one by air. All different destinations as well."

Kelly stopped midstride, processing what she'd heard. "You got hits on known aliases for *all four* members of their unit? In the span of an hour?"

"Yes, ma'am."

How odd, and not a good-luck kind of odd.

One member slipping up using a known alias was possible. She'd buy that and check it out, but all four was more than suspect. There was zero chance that the entire team would take such a gamble, and Hunter wouldn't be caught in such a stupid mistake. Not when they had time to prepare that ambush and escape without a trace.

This was deliberate, calculated. Topaz was trying to throw them off.

"I'm sending the information to your tactical team on the ground, Beta, as we speak," Ebony said.

It was protocol for the analysts to follow up on such leads, and Kelly appreciated initiative, but not in this case.

She hit the call button for the elevator. "No, don't do that." It would send her strike team on a wild-goose chase, which she suspected was the point. "The odds of this lead panning out are slim to none."

Hunter wanted them chasing after their tails instead of after him.

"I concur with that assessment, ma'am, and wouldn't have contacted the tactical team, but SAC Chief Clark asked me to."

"Come again?" Surely Kelly had misheard the woman. "When did you speak to Clark?"

"A few minutes ago, ma'am. After you and I spoke, the SAC chief called me and asked me to report all updates to him first. In fact, he said there was no need to apprise you of this because you were swamped and he'd handle it, but I thought it best for me to call you regardless."

Anger flooded through her. "When did Clark give you the instructions to notify him first?"

Ebony gave the precise time.

Kelly had been in a vehicle separate from Andrew on the way back to the hotel when that dirtbag tried to cut her out of the loop on her operation.

"I've documented everything, ma'am," she said, and Kelly was reminded why she had chosen this particular analyst.

Not someone beholden to Clark, who would forget to annotate the little things.

"Thank you. As I've said, do not pursue this. It isn't a lead. It's a diversion," Kelly said. "And good work. Keep it up. But from here on out, you call me regarding this matter and only me. I'll deal with Clark."

"Yes, ma'am."

Kelly put her phone away and collected herself, checking her reflection in the steel doors. She smoothed back her chignon, making sure her hair was in place.

The elevator chimed, and the doors opened.

Andrew was inside the car, holding the handle of his suitcase. He flashed a tense grin, looking as cagey and untrustworthy as ever.

Kelly adopted a composed smile—calm, pleasant, tempered and aloof—not hinting at the fury boiling in her veins. Releasing the handle of her hard-shell carry-on, she turned to the marines. "Would you catch the next one and, if you wouldn't mind, please bring my bag down with you."

"Of course, ma'am." One of them took her bag.

Kelly stepped inside the elevator next to Andrew. They had a long, colorful history together, and she was familiar with the man's capabilities as well as his weaknesses. She was going to exploit that to teach him a lesson.

The doors closed and the car went into motion, headed down.

"The secondary strike team is here, waiting in the lobby for me to give them their instructions," she said without mentioning she'd spoken to the analyst.

Andrew was in the dark. Precisely where she wanted him to stay.

"I'm sure they'll get a lead that'll help them track down the team. Surely Topaz is trying to get out of the country. Beta team should check the manifests of the trains, buses, boats, airlines. Leave no stone unturned."

"That is one idea. But I think I'll send them in a different direction." What that direction was, she had yet to figure out.

"It's standard protocol, and it makes the most sense for Topaz to run. You would be wise to listen to my advice. I should be the one leading the Beta team as is. A recommendation I'll make to the director."

So, that was his angle.

"Your advice holds about as much value as a can of poppycock." She let her smile widen, meeting his eyes in the reflection of the shiny doors, wanting to rile him up because he would let his anger override common sense. And he deserved it after pulling that little stunt with the analyst. All the while she paced herself, timing this tête-à-tête to perfection.

The elevator stopped.

"You're a little man with little ideas, Andrew."

The chime sounded.

"If you were wise, you'd stay in your lane before you get mowed down," she continued.

The doors opened.

"I'd hate to see you reduced to roadkill." Kelly stepped forward.

Andrew snatched her arm, jerking her to a stop as he called her the foulest thing one could say to a woman, loud enough to draw attention. But he didn't stop there. "The higher you climb, the harder you'll fall." He tightened his grip, squeezing to intentionally hurt her. "You don't know half as much as you think you do. You'd better watch your mouth and the way you speak to me, or I'll make you regret it."

Kelly caught the gaze of the other marines in the lobby, who were already in motion to assist to her, as well as those on Beta team, to be sure she had witnesses who'd seen that Andrew had put his hand on her in an aggressive manner first.

Then she pivoted, raising the arm that he had snatched up in front of her. She locked her other hand under his wrist, bending and rotating it along with his entire arm. A light kick to the side of his leg at the knee, not hard enough to break a bone, had him crumpling to the floor of the elevator. His wrist and shoulder were wrenched at a painful angle, and his face was twisted in agony.

"If you ever put your hand on me again, I will break it. Do you understand?"

"Y-yeah, yeah, let me go, Kelly." The fear in his eyes told her that her message had been received.

She dropped his wrist and gave her suit jacket a tug at the hem. He clutched his arm to his chest like a wounded animal.

Andrew hated her because she'd been promoted over him to deputy director. It didn't help that she was four years younger, even though she had more experience. The crux of his problem was her sex. She hadn't realized it until her godmother had pointed it out to her. Andrew was never condescending to male colleagues, never called them vulgar names no matter how incensed he became. And in all the years she'd worked with him, she'd never seen him grab another man's arm.

At least he'd think twice before touching her again.

When she turned back around, several marines were in front of the elevator with their hands on the hilts of their weapons. "Are you okay, ma'am?" one asked her.

"I'm fine. But he might need assistance." She hiked a thumb back at Andrew, who was still hissing in pain behind her, and strode off the elevator to Beta team.

Quinlan laughed as she approached him. The sound was dark and chilling. "Remind me never to get on your bad side."

The joke registered. She was no match for this man in any universe. He was six-two and pure muscle, but so was Hunter Wright, and she was fairly certain the outcome in a melee with Hunter wouldn't be a given. She'd learned how to fight an opponent who was bigger and stronger. The physical factor wasn't what would give Quinlan the winning edge.

The difference wasn't about skill or cunning. They were both highly trained.

It didn't even boil down to the fact that Quinlan was a brutal sociopath who lacked a conscience. Sure, he enjoyed his profession of killing and the only person he ultimately served was himself, but there was a darkness in him that frightened her.

Andrew had been right about one thing. If she was afraid, then everyone else should be quaking in their boots.

"I can take care of him for you." Quinlan gestured with his chin at Andrew, who was being helped out of the elevator. "Put him in a ditch where he'll never be found, and in the event that he is, he'll never be identified. I assure you."

As tempting as the idea was and as vexing as Andrew could be, that wasn't her style. He was still a colleague, even if she didn't respect him and he often got in her way. She didn't hire mercenaries to resolve a difficult working relationship.

The Topaz unit was a special case. She'd love nothing more than to bring them to justice and see the lot of them rot in a supermax prison. But they'd committed treason, killing a high-profile ally, had accepted payment to do so while acting under the guise of the CIA. Putting them on trial, airing dirty laundry along with government secrets and publicly tying the United States to that politically charged crime simply wouldn't happen. Could not happen under any circumstances.

Although she'd never admit it to anyone, this whole mess broke her heart.

Once such fine operatives. How had it come to this? How had Hunter strayed so far off course?

At her lack of an immediate response, Quinlan added, "I'd even cut you a discount. I never did like him."

"Thanks, but no, thanks. I can handle Andrew Clark."

"Yes, you can." Another grin from him that made her skin crawl.

She glanced around at the prying eyes. "Walk with me. Let's talk in the Suburban."

They left the air-conditioned lobby, briefly transiting through the heat.

"We're not to be disturbed by anyone, not even Clark," she said to the marine standing next to the vehicle before she climbed in and slid across the seat, making room for Quinlan.

He shut the door. "We received partial information from headquarters. Something about a train and a boat. Known aliases used. Do you want us to pursue it?"

"No. It would be a waste of your time."

Quinlan scrubbed a hand over his bald head. "Then what do you want us to do? They're not going to stick around in this country, that's for certain. An island was one thing. But here on the mainland where the surveillance is on steroids, they wouldn't last long," he said, and she had to agree. "Do you think they might try to go Stateside? Head back to Virginia?"

"Go home?"

She would've dismissed the idea as preposterous

eleven months ago. But since Gage and Dean had both been found in towns where they'd grown up, anything was a possibility. Zee had been hiding in a location that contradicted her profile, which had been smart, but still, she'd popped up on their radar as well.

What reason would they have to go back to Virginia?

That would be a huge risk for Topaz to take, and she couldn't see the potential reward.

"Go to the Cayman Islands," she said. "I'll send you the details about their offshore accounts. To our knowledge, some money has been withdrawn, but there's still quite a bit left just sitting there."

If they'd been so brazen as to set foot in the bank before, they'd do it again.

She'd seen video footage of Hunter waltzing into the bank, and the same day, a quarter of a million dollars had been withdrawn from his offshore account.

Almost as if he'd been thumbing his nose at her and the CIA, acting as though he were invincible. It only solidified her determination to catch Hunter and put an end to this travesty, which was a blight on the CIA's record.

"I'd also like you to leave a couple of men behind in Caracas," Kelly said. "To keep their fingers on the pulse of things and to make certain no one from Topaz is able to hide here."

"I'm one step ahead of you. I've reached out to a contact I have in the SEBIN," he said, referring to the internal security force of the repressive intelligence directorate of the country. "He'll keep an eye out. If Topaz pops up, he has men loyal to him who will eradicate the problem."

Quinlan was an outside-the-box thinker.

"Thank you." She gave a slight nod.

"No need to thank me. I'll send you the bill for this add-on."

Of course. Having an inside man in the Venezuelan intelligence service wouldn't be cheap, and Quinlan never acted out of the kindness of his heart.

"Your team should fly with us. We can drop you off." Getting the Beta team into Venezuela and geared up had been a logistical headache. Flying them private would be the most efficient way from here on out.

"Fine. It'll be faster to take the helo to the airport rather than drive, especially with all the attention we're garnering. Clark should ride with us. An open door, faulty seat buckle, a sharp turn—it's possible he takes a tumble and has a convenient accident."

The prospect horrified her.

Kelly plastered on a soft grin while gritting her teeth. "As much as I appreciate your resourcefulness and desire to go above and beyond, he's off-limits."

The corner of his mouth hitched up. "I bet when you return to Langley, you'll look back on this moment and wonder if you should've made a different choice." He chuckled. "No worries. You know my number in case you change your mind."

Andrew was a thorn in her side, right between the ribs. He would make things difficult in the days ahead. The man was an aggravation. Not a criminal or the enemy of the state.

What Quinlan proposed was revolting.

She would never regret doing the right thing.

They hopped out of the SUV to go back inside and take the elevator to the helipad on the roof. As she walked around the vehicle, a shiver skated over her, like a warm finger dipped in honey sliding down her spine.

She was being watched. Considering the circumstances and the gaggle of armed men around her, that wasn't unexpected.

What surprised her to the core was she had the sense that *he* was watching her. Kelly had only ever gotten that warm sensation when Hunter's gaze had been on her.

Remembering it, him, their time together in the office, in the hotel room, in bed together, sent a bittersweet ache seeping through her.

Whenever they had shared the same airspace, a bright, scorching heat flared to life.

What she felt now was more subtle, distant.

Was he really so reckless as to spy on her in Caracas? Or was she on edge with her senses misfiring?

Turning, she scanned the surrounding area.

PEERING THROUGH HIS SNIPERSCOPE, Hunter adjusted the sight, clarifying the image. He'd been desperate for more than a glimpse of her. Desperate to make her pay.

Now here she was in the flesh. In his crosshairs.

Kelly spun in a slow circle, her forehead creased in concentration as she looked around, giving him a 360-degree view of her, and his gut clenched.

Clad in a tailored ivory suit and wearing bone-colored

high heels that showed off her long, lithe legs, she was a vision to behold. Flaming red hair pulled up in an impeccable twist. Thinner than the last time he'd seen her, but her svelte figure was no less captivating. Her complexion was the same color as her suit. Softer. Luminous in the early-morning light.

Stopping, she angled her head in his direction, and he would've sworn that she looked right at him, through him.

His heart locked in his chest.

The odds she'd spotted him on the covered top floor of the nearby parking garage were nil. The sun was to his back, and there wasn't anything to cause a glare on his scope. Of that he was one hundred percent positive. With Zee on his right side and John, who had insisted on tagging along as a backup babysitter, at his left, they'd double-checked to be certain nothing gave away their position.

All Hunter needed to do was squeeze the trigger. Squeeze it and he could end her with one bullet.

His gaze was still trained on her, his finger caressing the trigger, his heart threatening to burst from his chest.

How had she gone from making love to him all night, wrapping herself around him, sharing her cold, dark past, fueling his belief that they'd shared a connection, to feeling nothing for him—besides the desire to see him dead?

"Our hands are tied here," Zee said, dragging him from his torturous thoughts. "She's with Quinlan and his men."

"A few marines would have been tricky, but doable.

This?" John grunted. "No way. I'm sorry, Hunter. Going after her here and now is a no-go."

Zee put a firm hand on his shoulder. "She's untouchable."

No one was untouchable. He could reach out with a bullet and touch her right now.

But then he'd never get answers. Never know why.

Without Kelly, he didn't have a chance at tracking down irrefutable evidence that she had set them up. In order to have a future and prevent more teams from coming after them, they had to clear their names.

He had no choice but to let her live. It was the only reason he didn't open fire.

Or so he told himself.

He needed the truth and the proof to substantiate it. He was resolved to be as cold and merciless as necessary in finding it.

Hunter's scope was still locked on her as he watched her.

Quinlan must have said something to Kelly, because she glanced at him as though her attention had been broken. Her lips moved. She gave one last look around before walking into the building with her armed entourage.

Hunter lowered the rifle.

Zee and John were right. For now, there was nothing he could do, even with their help.

But Kelly Russell wouldn't have bodyguards with her 24/7.

Sooner or later, there would be an opportunity to

get his hands on her and make her talk. When that happened, he'd be ready to seize it.

"What do you want to do?" Zee asked.

The battle for the day had been won, but those men who had stormed the island were merely foot soldiers. The real war was with Kelly and, by extension, the CIA. It could only be fought in Northern Virginia.

They had to leave Venezuela.

Hunter drew in a heavy breath. "It's time for us to go home."

Chapter Six

Giving her father's ring one final twist on her finger, Kelly crossed her legs at the ankle, seated before the director. She folded her hands in her lap, her back ramrod straight, her expression reserved despite the exhaustion and worry pressing down on her.

Andrew was in the chair beside her, being his usual eager, predictable self. "Did she tell you that she contracted that psycho Mickey Quinlan to head up her Beta team?" Agitation was stamped on his face, his voice hoarse with anger and fatigue. "The man is unhinged. There is an unspoken rule that we aren't to work with him. That alone should tell you she's not exercising sound judgment. She's shooting from the hip in desperation."

Director Price's gaze swung to her. "I'm inclined to agree with Andrew. In light of Quinlan's history, I'm having a hard time understanding this decision, Kelly. He leaves a bloody mess wherever he goes."

"My choice is somewhat unorthodox, I admit." As Price stared at her with his gray eyes, waiting patiently for her to say more, she sat taller and drew a breath.

"But it was one I had to make. I didn't have the opportunity to choose the primary strike team or to sign off on them. Look how that turned out."

Andrew shifted uncomfortably in his seat. "The only reason they weren't successful is because her—" he jabbed a finger in her direction "—former team got one up on us."

"Topaz did." Kelly gave a curt nod. "Because the reconnaissance executed by the Predator crew was compromised. They were given incompetent instructions from a higher-up." Not once had she spoken Andrew's name, or glanced at him, and she definitely hadn't pointed a finger like a five-year-old having a tantrum. "They should've been flying at twelve thousand feet with a standoff of two nautical miles. Those are the instructions I would've given them, but my authority was infringed upon. Topaz must have spotted the drone before the strike team's arrival. That's how they knew we were coming."

From her therapy sessions with her father as a teenager, she'd learned to use *I* statements and to stick with the facts. It was a communication strategy that was less accusatory and allowed for the actual issue to be clearly defined and addressed.

"The Predator mission commander should have known better." Andrew stabbed the arm of his chair as he spoke. "They do this all the time, tracking terrorists. This was no different."

"Until someone made it different by telling them they could disregard normal mission parameters because it didn't matter. Sir, really, is this the drone crew's fault?"

Price clenched his jaw as his gaze slid to Andrew.

"It's her fault," Andrew snapped. "Come on, we both know that. Everyone in this building knows it. I get that she's your favorite pet and you're grooming her to take over someday, but I think this proves she's not up for the task of executing Operation Cujo, much less running this place."

"I'm flabbergasted by this hostility toward me." Sighing with a disappointed shake of her head, she held the director's gaze. "This is the twenty-first century. I'd like to believe this organization won't tolerate the presence of violent misogynists who are incapable of controlling themselves."

"Violent!" Andrew jumped to his feet. "Do you know what this bitch did to me in the hotel elevator? She nearly broke my wrist. Go on, tell him about that."

Language, Andrew.

She didn't have to say a word. The director was well-informed.

Before they'd taken off from Simón Bolívar International, she'd had every single marine who had witnessed what had transpired in the elevator send an email to their immediate supervisor documenting it, and one went so far as to call. Marines worked round the clock. Surely their lieutenant colonel had reached out to the director posthaste.

"You need to calm down," the director said to him.

"Name-calling, the vulgarity." Kelly dropped her gaze to her father's ring. "I find it offensive. This kind of behavior only serves to create a hostile work environment."

"Sit down." The director gestured at Andrew. "And do yourself a favor by shutting up."

Andrew balked, but he lowered himself, silently, into the chair.

"Kelly is spearheading Operation Cujo," the director said, "but she asked to do it alone. You came crying to me, Andrew, wanting to dip your fingers in the pie and get a slice of the success. Well, you mucked things up. The waters are so blurry now, I don't know if she would've accomplished it without your interference. What I do know is that you have been more of a hindrance to her than a help. You are to take a back seat on this going forward and stay out of her way."

"But I should be leading Beta team. I'm the one—"

The director raised his palm. "And I don't ever want you to use such inappropriate language with a colleague. Right now, I'm not sure who is more unhinged, you or Quinlan."

"Sir," Andrew said on an exhale, making the one syllable sound as if it was deflating.

"Take a couple of days off. Go home. Cool down. Spend some time with your wife. Focus on other things in your life that are important."

His wife had left him six months ago, and Andrew was trying to keep it quiet. He didn't have anyone to go home to.

Then again, neither did Kelly, and the twinge from that emptiness was with her every time she entered her house.

"Work would really be the best thing for me," Andrew said. "I just need a little sleep and I'll be right as rain."

"It wasn't a suggestion." There was an awkward pause as Price stared at him with pity. "That was an order. Go home, why don't you? You never take leave and you've spent years working hours you've never claimed. I don't want you back in this building for seventy-two hours unless you're summoned. Understood?"

Slowly, reluctantly, Andrew nodded and stood. "I want it on the record that I think she shouldn't remain in charge of Operation Cujo. She's unfit."

"Okay. Sure." Price gave him a sympathetic nod. "I will document your personal feelings."

"Not personal feelings. My professional assessment."

"If you push this, then I'll have to document other things. Such as the aggressive behavior you just displayed in my office and your foul language directed at a coworker. Your superior, no less. I'm trying to help you out here. Go home. Get some rest. Enjoy the time with that beautiful wife of yours, and tell Leslie I said hi."

Without a word, Andrew skulked out of the office. Beaten. Tail between his legs.

Kelly actually felt bad for him, even though she shouldn't. He'd behaved horribly, but she understood some of what he might be feeling in this moment beyond the defeat.

She was a workaholic, too. Without this job, this place, what did she have?

The same thing Andrew had. Absolutely nothing.

They sacrificed everything for this job, and not once did she ever question if the heavy toll was worth it.

This was for the greater good of this country, for national security, to make the world a better, safer place. Someone had to do it. Her father had raised her to do this and ensured she had the perfect skill set to be successful.

"Can you handle this?" Price asked her.

"Yes," she said unequivocally, though doubt rattled through her.

She had no choice but to handle it. Everything was on the line. She could not afford to make another mistake. The gamble was that Topaz would mess up before she did. No one was perfect. No matter how much talent they had, everyone got tripped up. To complicate the odds for her, Topaz wasn't working alone. They had assistance from a former Navy SEAL and two civilians. The SEAL worried her. He'd proven to be a formidable force when the CIA had sent a team after Zee.

While Kelly only had herself to rely on.

"I believe in you," Price said. "Don't prove me wrong. You won't survive the scrutiny a second time around if this op goes south."

He didn't mean her career. She'd barely survived eleven months ago. Guilt by association until proven innocent was the way it worked in the hallowed halls of Langley. The one thing that'd saved her had been admitting to her onetime indiscretion with Hunter immediately after it had happened. If their night together had come out in a polygraph in the aftermath of Topaz's treasonous act, she would've been done for.

With a nod, she acknowledged him and stood, smoothing down her skirt.

Then he added, "We can't risk any exposure on this. If Quinlan wreaks havoc, crosses the line, it will fall solely on you."

She wouldn't have it any other way. Theirs was not a risk-free business, and she had rolled the dice on Quinlan. "I'll take full responsibility for his actions. I chose him."

"That you did. Be careful."

"I always am."

IN FAIRFAX, VIRGINIA, Hunter and the others were getting settled in the closest thing to an unofficial safe house. Zee had arranged their lodgings. The woman was not only a genius but also a magician. With a few clicks on her laptop, she'd found a nearly vacant, no-frills budget motel with limited CCTV coverage that was willing to take cash for a short-term stay without asking too many questions. The best part was the location. She'd rented a block of rooms to ensure their privacy, and they had quick, easy access to both I-66 and I-495. In the span of a short drive, they could be in McLean, where Langley was located.

The rental of a private Cessna to take the team from Venezuela to a landing strip just outside Fairfax County had eaten up a significant chunk of the cash they had left. The motel rooms had been cheap in comparison, but their hard currency was dwindling. They weren't strapped by any means. Zee had started investing in Bitcoin a few years back and had done remarkably well. The cryptocurrency was in an account the CIA wasn't aware of, because they'd gone into hiding before her next financial disclosure had been due, but they had a problem. Most people didn't take digital currency as payment. The pilot had wanted cash. The hotel wanted cash or a credit card. Sorry, no Bitcoin accepted.

Digital currency ATMs weren't so easy to find abroad. On American soil was a different story. She could tap one thirty minutes away. But Zee was an ethical hacker. She hadn't tried to hide her identity when she'd created the account. As soon as she made a withdrawal, the CIA would pick it up. Then there was the issue of anyone getting close to an ATM due to security cameras.

They had to be cognizant of all CCTV.

Every move they made had to be careful, calculated.

The slightest misstep would put them in a bind at best. At worst, it could cost them their lives.

With the eight of them crammed into one room to talk, tension was dense as fog. Everyone felt it in varying degrees, especially the civilians in their forged family. Kate, a veterinarian turned into their resident doctor, was used to a slower pace and the security of a small town. Danger was nothing new to Hope, a photojournalist who had often found herself in precarious situations for a job. But neither was accustomed to this grueling high-ops tempo with threats around every corner.

Olivia might be a child, but Zee had trained and prepared her to handle this type of pressure.

Hunter wanted to keep the three of them as far removed as possible. He didn't want them being used as leverage or put in harm's way.

If he could accomplish this on his lonesome and clear

their names without jeopardizing any of his people, he would.

"Is everyone clear on the next step?" Hunter asked.

Heads nodded around the room.

"I'll need Zee to come along to handle the alarm system," he said, "and one more person." The backup would be essential in this case.

John stepped forward. "I'll go."

"No, you have to stay here." Zee put a hand on his broad chest. "I thought about it on the flight. I need one of us to always be with Olivia from here on out. In the event things take a turn for the worse—"

"We can't think like that," John said.

A sad smile tugged at Zee's mouth. "But we have to."

Olivia climbed off one of the double beds where she was sitting and went up to John and her mother. "I'll be okay with everyone else. Isn't it better for you, Mom, if John goes?"

John would put Zee above everything, even at the expense of their last-ditch mission to clear their names. He wasn't Hunter's first or second pick to go.

"It's better for you, sweetheart, if one of us stays," Zee said to her daughter. "That way, no matter what, you'll be taken care of."

The subject was hard to tiptoe around, the prospect of things not working out in their favor. The possibility of this ending with a funeral instead of a celebration. Hunter admired their efforts to try as well as the courageous way Olivia was facing this.

Not many men would embrace the challenge of having an instant family. John had accepted Olivia as his own, and Zee knew that he would love and protect that little girl for the rest of his life.

"Okay. I'll stay." John wrapped one arm around Zee, the other around Olivia and kissed each of them on the head.

Looking at the three of them, huddled together, was enough to make a cynic like Hunter believe in destiny and true love and hope they got their happily-ever-after. They deserved it. As did the other two couples in the room.

Before Gage could offer to go, Dean did. "I'll be the third."

Gage, never one to shirk duty, was about to protest, but Hope took his hand and caught his gaze.

"The three of us will handle it," Hunter said to reassure Gage. "You should stay."

Gage and Hope hadn't had a chance to talk privately since the baby bombshell. Taking some time to decompress, to process the news that they were expecting, was important. They had to seize any moment for normalcy when feasible.

Nodding, Gage interlaced his fingers with Hope's.

"If we're not back in four hours or if you haven't heard from us…" Hunter stopped short of saying *you should assume we are dead* in front of Olivia. The insinuation was clear.

They would be on their own and would have to run. Limited cash would make it tough until they could access Zee's crypto savings, but Hunter was leaving them with everything they had left.

"Just make sure it doesn't come to that," John said, hiding his concern behind a hardened warrior's stare.

"I'll do my best," Hunter said, hoping that his best would be good enough.

Almost two days with no sleep, and Kelly had hit a mental wall. She hadn't been able to rest on the flights to or from Venezuela, and after talking with Director Price, she'd gathered her team of analysts.

Quinlan had discovered all the accounts in the Cayman Islands had been emptied through wire transfers and closed. With nothing else to go on, he was headed back Stateside. Kelly had pushed her analysts for the past several hours to figure out where the members of Topaz would go. Would they stay together? Would they separate to make it harder to find them?

They were stitching together everything they knew about them from their profiles and history, in conjunction with their current behavior and the information they'd dug up on their collaborators: Hope Fischer, John Lowry and Kate Sawyer.

From there they would extrapolate, because other than getting false positives on the use of their known aliases, they had nothing else to go on. Not a single hit on facial recognition.

Either they were hiding off the grid somewhere or Zee was keeping them from being detected using her ace hacker skills. Or it was a combination of both.

Pinching the bridge of her nose as she squeezed her eyes shut, Kelly realized she had to pack it in for a few hours. Go home. Take a shower. Get some rest and food. Then come back and tackle this with a fresh perspective.

"I'm heading home," she said to the analysts who had done a shift change before dinner. "If you find anything, notify me and only me immediately."

"Yes, ma'am."

She grabbed her overcoat and purse and left the private operations room where Cujo was being conducted. Others steered clear of her in the halls, and no one initiated conversation in the elevator. Her reputation as the ice queen was well-known. People feared her. Most days that didn't bother her, but what she would've given to have an ally. A friend on her side.

Once this was resolved, she'd take a few days of leave. Maybe spend the vacation with her godmother. Judith had managed to juggle a husband for a decade when she was younger, and the marriage had given her a son, Zachary, who was five years older than Kelly. Somehow, he had turned out easygoing, content with a nine-to-five job as the head of public affairs at the NSA.

The vacation would probably come down to Kelly and Zach. Judith stayed busy, rarely had time for herself. Then she'd be stuck with Mr. Mellow, who never stressed about anything and didn't understand the pressures of a high-powered position. He was a nice guy. The big brother she never had. They were simply cut from a different cloth.

Perhaps Kelly would retreat to her godmother's house in West Virginia. Fresh air. Good wine. Great food. And she could enjoy it alone.

Always alone.

Ignoring the sting of emptiness, she passed security as she crossed the lobby and left the building. One perk of her position was a nearby parking spot. With color-coded lots befitting Disneyland, the benefit was nothing to scoff at. She hurried to her car and climbed inside, out of the cold.

On her way home, some of the tension dissipated, draining from her shoulders. But the knot in the pit of her stomach refused to loosen. Her hands tightened on the steering wheel. A storm of emotions swirled inside her. Anger, frustration, loneliness, uncertainty, regret.

If only she'd seen the warning signs that Topaz might turn traitor, maybe she could have prevented things from getting to this point.

Regardless, their fates were linked now.

Hitting the button to open her garage, she pulled up the driveway of her home in Vienna. The four-bedroom brick colonial where she grew up. Her father had bequeathed her the house in excellent condition with the mortgage paid off to ensure she wouldn't have to worry about money.

Even in death he looked out for her.

She turned off the ignition, closed the garage door, got out of the car and entered the house.

The alarm chirped. Kelly entered the four-digit PIN, turning it off, and dead bolted the door.

Rolling her shoulders and stretching her neck, she strode down the short, narrow hall. She dumped her purse and keys on the entry table and entered the kitchen.

A second before she spotted him, she sensed him. That warm finger sliding down her spine.

Hunter Wright stood in the moonlight on the opposite side of her kitchen island, waiting for her.

For a long moment, they both simply stood and stared. The air between them vibrated with an awareness that was nearly palpable.

Painful memories sliced through her brain in a rush. Late nights in the office, side by side. Flirting disguised as witty repartee. That TDY in Boston. The taste of his mouth. The smell of his skin. The feel of his body on her. Inside her.

She struggled to breathe, her lungs squeezing, her heart throbbing like an open wound.

Then a surge of adrenaline had her springing into action. She spun around, lunging for the entry table. Yanked open the drawer where she kept a loaded nine-millimeter Glock. Grabbed the handgun and whirled as she thumbed off the safety.

She aimed center mass. The way her father had taught her. Not at the limbs or the head, and she certainly didn't want to mess up that gorgeous face of his. The man had won the genetic lottery big-time and deserved an open casket.

Hitting a target was harder than it looked on TV or in movies. So she pointed the gun at his chest, where a bullet was likely to strike the aorta, the vena cava, a lung, the spine.

She drew closer, the click of her heels on the wood floor the only sound in the room.

Out of all the places in the world he could've gone, he was in her house. Before she pumped him full of lead, she'd find out why.

"Raise both hands, slowly, where I can see them." She stopped, close enough to strike her target, but with distance between them to prevent him from disarming her.

He moved his arms, bringing his hands into sight, both clenched into fists. Once he reached his torso, he froze, only a second. Then he opened his hands.

Bullets fell from his palms, raining down on the marble countertop. "I found the Glock and the Beretta while I was waiting."

Damn it. He'd unloaded both.

But maybe he'd forgotten the round she kept chambered.

Kelly squeezed the trigger. *Click!* She threw the gun at his head, cursing the fact she was in a stupid skirt. It would limit her range of motion in a fight. She could put more power behind a well-placed kick than a punch.

Nonetheless, she could still knee his groin, and there was nothing like a stiletto heel to a kneecap to make someone feel blinding agony.

Hunter stalked around the counter toward her, moving like a predator.

It was unnerving and sexy as hell at the same time.

She raised her fists and widened her stance. "Come on. I'll teach you not to break into my house."

The floorboards creaked and groaned under shifting weight. *Behind her.*

Kelly's whole body flashed cold as the realization occurred to her that Hunter hadn't come alone.

She pivoted to turn, but someone slipped an arm around her throat, locking her in a choke hold.

Stalking closer, Hunter smiled, so brazen, so cock-sure, as though certain he had her.

Kelly kicked off the kitchen island in front of her, sending her and the second assailant stumbling back and crashing into a table. Slamming the spike of her stiletto onto his foot, she used every ounce of force she could muster.

A guttural curse left his mouth, and his arm slackened around her throat from the unexpected jab of pain. Kelly unlocked her knees and sank down, grabbing the man's forearm with both hands. Then she bent forward at the waist with a sudden jerk, sending him flying over her head and to the floor.

Dean Delgado.

Two against one. They should be ashamed of themselves.

She stomped her heeled foot in his midsection, bearing down with her full weight.

Howling in pain, Dean grabbed his stomach. After she dealt with Hunter, her next kick would be to Dean's throat.

Hunter was almost on her now, crossing the kitchen.

She leaped over Dean's writhing body and dropped to a knee just as Hunter swung for her and missed. She threw a fist to his groin. Once he doubled over from the sucker punch, she rammed the heel of her palm up into his face, driving him backward.

A shadow slipped into her peripheral vision. A third person.

Kelly whirled, scrambling to her feet—too late. She caught sight of Zee and then the electric-blue sparks of the Taser right before the crackling stun gun was thrust into her side. The sudden shock of voltage felt like being punched by a gorilla. Kelly's legs stopped working and she collapsed as the world went black.

Chapter Seven

At the motel, Hunter and Dean were still recovering from Kelly's attack.

Although Hunter only had a bloody nose, the memory of being struck between the legs and the agonizing pain that only a man understood was fresh in his mind.

Kate had determined that Dean had bruised ribs. It could have been worse. At least none were broken, and she hadn't punctured a lung. He was in his room resting now.

This was why Hunter had wanted a three-person team to subdue Kelly. The woman was not to be trifled with. If they hadn't taken the time to search her place for weapons, she would've shot them dead. Instead, she'd only beaten them up.

Humiliating as it was, that was the truth.

Hunter turned off the faucet of the tub, figuring there was enough tepid water in it. Stepping into the bedroom, he caught the handcuffs that Zee tossed his way. He shoved them into his back pocket.

Kelly lay on the king-size bed, unconscious from the light sedative they'd given her to keep her knocked out while they transported her to the motel. Zee had removed Kelly's suit, leaving her clad in her underwear and a slip. The mint-green satin chemise had lace trim around the neckline with the hem falling high above the knee. He was viscerally aware of her bare arms and legs, lean and toned.

The old tug toward her was still there. More of a hard yank, really, if he were being honest, and he hated it. Why couldn't he ignore his attraction to her?

There was a knock on the door before Gage entered the room, carrying two twenty-pound bags of ice and a plastic shopping bag.

They were ready for the next step.

Zee took Kelly's temperature with a forehead thermometer. "Every five minutes I'll check her to be sure her body temp doesn't drop too low."

Hunter gave a nod. Then he pushed up his sleeves to keep from getting his sweater wet and scooped Kelly up from the bed. Her head fell against his chest as he cradled her in his arms and walked into the bathroom. She was so warm and soft, he loathed feeling the slightest enjoyment from the contact, from her skin against his.

He took comfort in the fact that it would be short-lived. In the next minute, she'd be wide-awake, hissing and clawing like a wildcat, trying to kill him.

Gently, he eased her into the water, not wanting to hurt her—at least not physically, despite the whupping she'd given them. In her house, he'd swung at her with enough force to knock someone out, but he had doubted he'd would've been able to land a single blow.

Kelly was highly trained and fast, and he'd been right about her.

She stirred, groaning, her head rolling from side to side.

He took the handcuffs from his back pocket and slipped the chain around the safety grab bar bolted to the wall. Then he cuffed her wrists tightly to be sure she couldn't slip out of them. Her ankles were restrained with zip ties.

Nodding to Gage, Hunter gave him the go-ahead.

Gage brought the bags of ice into the bathroom. They each opened a bag and dumped the freezing contents into the tub.

With a sharp gasp, Kelly's eyes flew open. Her frantic gaze landed on them, and immediately she started jerking on the cuffs like it was possible for her to rip the metal bar from the wall.

"Might as well settle down, because you're not going anywhere." Not anytime soon.

"What's going on?" She jerked her arms again. "Where am I? What are you doing?" she demanded as though she were in charge of this situation.

"You're here to give us answers," Hunter said, calm and composed. It was going to take drastic measures. They were prepared to do what was necessary to get honest responses.

"If you wanted to chat, all you had to do was call. You've got my number. No need to ambush me in my own home. Three against one. Pathetic," Kelly said, her tongue sharp as ever, and damn if he didn't admire her spunk. "Cheaters. No honor. No shame. I should've expected nothing less. Couldn't even be man enough to fight me one-on-one."

Swallowing his frustration and anger, he clenched a hand. "This needs to be done face-to-face. So I can tell when you're lying." Reflecting on it in hindsight, everything that had come out of her mouth had probably been lies. He needed to see her eyes to tell when she was speaking the truth.

Kelly barked out a scathing laugh. "Is this just a pitiful excuse to get my clothes off again?"

"You seduced me," Hunter said, "not the other way around."

"Is that how you remember it? Guess our recollections differ."

Hunter turned to Gage and Zee, who both stood silent, observing, analyzing everything. "Out. Both of you."

"What about the interrogation?" Zee asked. "We should be here for it."

"Interrogation?" Kelly laughed again, shivering from the ice bath. "Is this supposed to be some kind of torture? It'll do wonders for my pores." Another chuckle rolled from her pink lips. "I've already been through real torture thanks to this traitorous little unit. Did you know they took me to a black site after you all went rogue?"

"Oh, please." Hunter sighed, kneeling beside the tub with an arm propped on his thigh. "Is that what you call a promotion these days, torture?"

"Everyone thought I had taken vacation days until the dust settled." Her face took on a feral sort of look, her eyes becoming catlike. "I was getting a tan under hot, bright lights I had sweltered under while they played loud heavy metal music to keep me awake. No swimming, I'm afraid, but they did waterboard me a few times. I only got a break from it during the polygraphs. Over and over. To be sure I wasn't a no-good traitor like the rest of you. So have at it. Give this your best shot, because once I get free, I'm going to kill *all* of you."

She would most certainly try, and they were prepared for that, too.

Hunter stared at her, studying her. "You must be the only person in history to leave a black site and get a promotion. To deputy director."

"Price has been grooming me. The promotion was given to me early as an apology for the torture once I proved my innocence."

Hunter considered what she had to say. It was a good story, definitely intriguing while invoking the right note of sympathy for her. Too bad it was a lie. Kelly was Scheherazade and knew how to spin a good tale. She'd run them around in circles all night if given the chance. They had a limited window to get answers.

The deputy director of the CIA couldn't go missing for days on end. They had hours before someone started looking for her.

Hunter held out his hand to Zee. "Give it to me."

Zee pulled a syringe from her pocket and placed it in his palm.

Hunter flicked off the cap and tapped the tube to get out the air bubbles.

Alarm flared in Kelly's eyes as she jerked back. "What is that?"

"Something I picked up in Venezuela. Better than sodium pentothal." It was an ultra-short-acting psychoactive drug used to obtain information from those who were unwilling to give it. The stuff caused consistent and predictable truth-telling. Combined with the ice bath to enhance the effects, no one could lie. Kelly was about to spill her guts. Hunter leaned forward with the hypodermic needle, and Kelly began thrashing in the tub. "I've got more of this, plenty of other needles, and I can have Gage and Zee hold you down. Fighting this is pointless."

Kelly clenched her jaw and stiffened, accepting there was no avoiding this.

Hunter injected her in the arm and depressed the plunger. "I'll handle this alone," he said to Zee and Gage.

"We're staying to hear the answers." Zee stood her ground, and he wondered if that was the real reason.

"I'm not going to kill her." Not yet anyway. First, he needed proof of their innocence.

"I agree with Zee," Gage said. "We stay. But we can hang back a bit in here to give you space to work."

That was as good as it was going to get. They were both afraid to leave him alone with Kelly. Maybe he couldn't be trusted for more than one reason—half of him wanted to strangle her, and the other half wanted to kiss her.

"Fine," Hunter gritted out.

They moved into the bedroom, staying close to the

open bathroom door, where they could hear without being seen.

Hunter turned back to Kelly. The drug was taking effect. Her pupils were dilated, and she looked woozy despite the cold making her teeth chatter.

"Where were we?" he asked.

Her cobalt blue eyes narrowed to slits. "Discussing how pathetic you are. If stripping me and getting me wet was what you were after—"

"In your dreams, sugar."

There was nothing sweet about Kelly. She was all fire and secrets. He preferred the heat of her passion over her wrath, but right now he was after those secrets.

"More like in your fantasies, I bet." She rested her head back against the wall.

"Don't flatter yourself."

"I don't have to. You already did. Remember? That one night. TDY. Boston." She licked her lips, and he re-called the feel of her mouth on him, their tongues tan-gled, the sweet heat that'd blazed through him, melting away all his defenses.

Hours of pleasure, lost in each other, but it had been more than that, at least for him. The sense of connec-tion, that feeling of hope, had been everything. In the euphoria of their lovemaking, he had flattered her. The words had been genuine. Heartfelt.

Thinking back on it brought him nothing but misery.

"After I'd had too many drinks," she added, "and you seduced me."

The drugs must not have fully kicked in yet if she

was still running with the lie that he had been the one acting from a playbook.

"I vaguely remember the night," he said, sounding bored, but the memory of the way her body had moved beneath him, over him, dominating and surrendering, was burned in his mind when none of it had meant anything to her. He put the mental brakes on, refusing to go there any deeper. "But it sounds as if you recall everything in vivid detail."

"Oh, please," she scoffed. "Of course I do. Retaining information is part of the job."

"That's all I ever was to you. A job. A tool to be used. Like a hammer."

"You once had the precision of a scalpel. Until Afghanistan. When you took money and turned traitor. Betrayed your country. Betrayed me."

He grasped her chin between his thumb and forefinger, turning her face to his. She stared at him until, after a long moment, she took a shuddering breath.

"You've got that backward." His voice was low and hard. "You set us up with that op. You were the one who betrayed *us*."

She had picked their team for the mission in Afghanistan. She had verified the target, which, in the end, had been the wrong man. She was the one who had arranged their exit plan out of country. And all of it had gone to hell in a handbasket.

To make matters worse, when they'd finally made their way back to the United States and asked her to meet them so they could find out what in the world had gone wrong, a kill team turned up. They'd barely gotten away and had been forced to go on the run.

Kelly had ruined their reputations and destroyed their lives like it had been a game of climb the ladder to her. It brought him to a level of rage that he hadn't experienced in a long time.

"Is this sick joke part of the torture?" She pulled her chin out of his grasp. "I was horrified by what you did. Not just against this country. Against the agency. But…" She lowered her gaze and shook her head as if trying to clear it.

"But?" he prodded. "Don't hold back now. You never have before with your lies and manipulation."

"You betrayed me!" She stared up at him with glassy eyes. "Not the other way around. When you went rogue, Hunter, you broke my heart. I believed in you. Thought I could count on you. I trusted you more than anyone." Her bottom lip quivered as a whimper escaped her.

He couldn't tell if the wounded sound was from the cold or something else. Then she went on.

"Do you know how hard that was for me?" Her voice was tight, ragged with emotion. Deep, strong, real emotion that astounded him. "God, I thought I was f-fall…" Shaking her head again, she pressed her lips together.

"You thought you were what?"

"It doesn't matter! Not anymore. It stopped being important the day you betrayed me and left me behind. To be humiliated. To be interrogated. To be judged. For what you all did." She bared her teeth and growled, but tears leaked from the corners of her eyes. "I want to wrap my hands around your throat and choke the life out of you."

He'd been so angry for so long he hadn't allowed himself to feel much else.

Now, a sudden swell of pain surged through him, knocking Hunter back on his heels. His chest ached. His throat burned. He hadn't expected to feel *this*.

Even without the drug, he would've believed her. Never, not once in all the days he'd known her, had Kelly let her icy control slip enough to show such gut-wrenching vulnerability.

The sight of this strong, fearless woman in tears frightened him.

Zee came to the doorway. "It's a little past five minutes, but I didn't want to interrupt."

He waved her in.

Zee put the handheld device to Kelly's forehead and scanned her. Once it beeped, she glanced at the screen. "You're good to keep going, but not for much longer." She left the room.

Hunter swallowed hard, watching Kelly shiver and sob in the ice bath. "Were you really tortured?"

"For seven days." She looked up at him. Her gaze open, glassy, wounded. "While you were on a lurid, postcard-perfect beach off the coast of Venezuela— golden sand, aquamarine sea, enjoying your freedom and the money you took to kill an innocent man."

These past eleven months he'd sworn it had been Kelly. It was the only thing that made sense. But this left him with more questions than answers.

"If you didn't set us up to murder the Afghan official,

then why didn't you show up after I contacted you for a meeting? Why did a kill team come for us instead?"

Confusion swamped her face. "What meeting? I don't know what you're talking about."

"I sent you a text from a burner phone. Used our code that no one else knew. You confirmed the meet. But you didn't come. You sent a hit squad."

"No." Kelly shook her head. "I never got any text. You never contacted me. I would've come. To hear your explanation before I slapped your face." She jerked her hands, the cuffs clinking against the bar. "How could you think I would ever set you up? I was your handler! Your advocate! I defended you until I was forced to accept the truth."

This was no act to disguise her guilt. She really did believe they were traitors, that they had become hired guns. Turned on their country, on her, for money.

Zee came back into the bathroom and scanned Kelly's forehead. "We've got to get her out and warm her up." Drawing in a deep breath, Zee shook her head. "It wasn't Kelly. She didn't do this to us."

He agreed. Hearing someone else acknowledge it had a tingle of relief loosening the fist that was around his heart.

But if Kelly hadn't set them up, then who had?

"I need one more minute with her," Hunter said to Zee.

"Sixty seconds. No longer."

He nodded. Thirty would suffice. "I'm going to take you out of the tub," he said to Kelly. "Give me your word that when I uncuff you, you won't get violent."

"I won't attack anyone." Her voice was throaty and trembling. "Not until this drug wears off."

That he believed, and it was good enough for him. The psychoactive drug affected the central nervous system. Even if she did try to attack them, she wouldn't be able to do much damage, but he didn't want the hassle of fighting with her.

He unlocked the cuffs and removed the restraint from one wrist. She grasped hold of the grab bar and lifted herself up. He reached for her to help her out of the tub, but she slapped his hand away.

Kelly managed to lurch out of the tub, shivering so hard she could barely stand.

Hunter caught her just as she started to fall, gripping her by her shoulders and holding her upright.

"Don't touch me." She jerked free of him and leaned against the counter.

Swearing under his breath, he forced himself not to go to her. She might appear weak and fragile, but it was temporary and didn't extend to her iron will.

Zee draped a towel around Kelly's shoulders and ran another one over her, drying her hair and legs.

Pushing off the counter, Kelly staggered and swayed. Her knees began to buckle, and all hesitation left him.

Hunter was by her side before she hit the floor and picked her up even though he knew she'd protest.

Instantly, she tensed and tried to twist out of his arms, but she lacked the strength to put up a real fight. There was no way she'd make it to the next room on her own.

"Hang on," he said, carrying her into the bedroom.

Her pale skin was freezing cold, which had been the point, and her teeth were still chattering. He regretted putting her through that, especially after learning what the CIA had done to her at a black site, but it had been the only way to find out the truth. "I'll put you down in just a second. I don't want to touch you any more than you want to be touched." It was a good thing for him that he wasn't under the truth serum. Now that he knew she wasn't responsible for what had happened to his team, nothing felt better than having her in his arms.

On the bed was a new pair of sweats that Gage had picked up from the store while he'd been out getting the ice. Hunter sat Kelly down on the edge of the bed next to the fresh clothes. Then he grabbed the thermos on the dresser that was filled with hot broth. It would warm her from the inside out.

"I'll help get her changed," Zee said, taking the thermos from his hand.

"I don't need your help, either." Kelly sat with her head hung, trembling, her hands clenched and shaking on her legs.

Zee sucked in a long, hard breath and exhaled in the same drawn-out manner.

Kelly's obstinacy knew no bounds.

"Suit yourself," Zee said, "but I'll hang around to supervise. Make sure you don't get any dangerous ideas."

Hunter gestured to Gage, and the two of them left the motel room and stood outside in the fresh air.

"All this time we've been blaming Kelly when she's not responsible," Gage said.

The thought of what she had gone through at a black

site had rage mixed with horror making his gut burn. He wanted to tear into whoever was responsible and rip them to shreds. They were still no closer to figuring out who that person was, and there were too many unanswered questions.

Deep down he sensed that somehow Kelly was the key to getting to the bottom of it.

"We need her help," Hunter said. "Someone on the inside to dig around."

A harsh breath left Gage's mouth, crystallizing in the air. "As if she'd help us now."

"I'll talk to her."

"Yeah, good luck with that. I'm pretty sure she hates us more now after that ice bath."

And the drugs. Kelly wouldn't let him forget that.

"She'll help." At Gage's skeptical expression, Hunter said, "She will." She had to, and Hunter believed that once he finally explained their side of the things, showed her what evidence they'd scraped together, that she would feel compelled.

He hoped like hell that was how it would work out. The bottom line, Kelly was a professional. She understood better than most at Langley the lengths an operative had to go to at times. If anyone would get the actions they'd taken tonight, his money was on her.

Zee opened the door, holding Kelly's wet things. "I'll get this stuff cleaned and dried."

"Thank you," Hunter said. "Do I have permission to speak to her alone?"

Zee gave him a rueful smile. "Sorry about that, but I needed to be sure."

"Of what?"

"That you wouldn't strangle her in a fit of rage. At least, not before we got answers, and now we've confirmed that she's innocent."

It was a great relief to know Kelly wasn't the enemy, but it did little to ease the tension knotted in his chest.

Hunter stepped inside the room. "Get some rest while you can."

"When are you going to sleep?" Gage asked.

"I'll sleep when I'm dead." Hunter closed the door, locked it and shoved a wedge-shaped rubber stopper under the door. An old habit from whenever he deployed.

With her back to him, Kelly was curled up on the bed in the fetal position under the covers.

He went to the dresser and pushed it in front of the door. That was to slow her down in the event she made a run for it once the drugs wore off and she got her strength back. They'd already unplugged the landline and hid the phone, and they'd made certain to leave both of her cell phones at her house.

There was no way for her to contact anyone. Not while she was in this room with him.

Hunter walked around to the other side of the bed and sank to the floor with his back pressed to the nightstand. The impact of hitting a brick wall rather than breaking through one hung in the air, settling on his shoulders.

Pulling his legs to his chest and resting his arms on his knees, he looked over at Kelly.

She was awake, so calm, clutching the covers to her chest. No doubt fuming on the inside.

Not that he blamed her.

"I'm sorry I put you through that." His voice was low and soft. "I had to be certain you told us the truth."

She was pale, hollow-eyed, and she didn't say a word.

The silence between them was dark and deep. He wanted to cross it. At the same time, he feared he never would. Finding a way to walk the line between the civility she deserved, now knowing she wasn't behind what happened to them, and the violence this path demanded seemed impossible.

Maybe this wasn't the right time to explain everything to her, present his argument of how they were innocent. It was better to wait until the drugs wore off. That way he could be certain her mind was clear to process everything.

But in this moment, with her unable to lie, there was one last thing he needed to know.

"In Boston," he said, hesitating a second, "if you didn't sleep with me to manipulate me, why did you seduce me on our last night?"

"You seduced me." Her voice was a whisper. "*And* I seduced you. I thought it had been mutual. That we'd wanted each other. You flirted. I flirted back. Gave you a chance to make a move. That's how I remember it."

Thinking that Kelly was the enemy had colored and framed so many things.

Everything.

His next question danced on his tongue, his pride making him reconsider whether to ask at all, but this was his one chance. He wanted, no, *needed* to know the truth. "Did you enjoy being with me, our one night together?"

She squeezed her eyes shut and tears leaked out, trickling down her cheeks. "Yes."

"Then why? Why were you so cold to me the next morning? Why did you leave the way that you did?"

"It doesn't matter. It was a year and a half ago."

"And here I sit. A fugitive, running for my life, and I'm still asking you. Whether it's been two years or twenty, it matters to me." He'd spent so many sleepless nights replaying that night, wondering, questioning. "Why?"

"Because I felt too much for you." She opened her eyes and shifted her sad gaze to his. "Not just the sex, which was amazing, but..." She trailed off and swallowed as though her throat hurt. "I was falling for you. Hard. I'd been into you for so long, and sleeping with you made it so much worse. It scared me." Tears starred her lashes. "I thought a clean break was for the best. That I was sparing us the pain of wanting something more, something we couldn't have. Not while we worked together."

He reached for her, slowly, and brushed her cheek with the back of his hand.

Just as he thought they were making a different kind of headway, she pulled back from his touch and rolled over, curling up on her side with her back to him.

After all this time, after the misconceptions, the lies, the fallacies on both sides, they were within arm's reach, but it might as well have been the Grand Canyon between them.

"I wish," he muttered. "I wish…" He wished so many things he didn't even know where to begin.

"Yeah," Kelly whispered, saving him from having to finish his statement. "Me, too."

If he had known back then, if she had taken ten minutes to tell him that had been the reason she'd acted as though she couldn't bear to be in the same room with him, he would've quit his job. Turned in his badge and gone to work as a contractor with his pick of security firms.

Then maybe none of this would've happened.

But she hadn't.

Kelly had chosen silence, the CIA and service before self over any chance of happiness with him.

The grim reality of the situation grabbed him by the throat, and he could barely breathe.

Now he needed Kelly to put him and his entire unit first. Ahead of the institution and principles that meant the most to her.

Otherwise, they'd never get exonerated, never be free. The eight of them couldn't run forever. They were operating on borrowed time.

Without her help, they'd never survive.

Chapter Eight

"Kelly." A deep, faraway voice tugged at her.

The sleep her body had craved for so long had her in its tight grip and wasn't letting go. She was warm, so tired. Needed to keep her eyes closed for just a little longer.

"Kelly." A rough shake accompanied the voice this time.

Sleep receded like an ebbing tide. She opened her eyes and Hunter came into focus.

He was crouched low next to the bed. Those piercing crystal-blue eyes were locked on her. His gorgeous face was so close she could touch him.

Then she remembered she wanted to smash that face to pieces. She jabbed out at him with a fist. Too slowly to do any damage. Unfortunately.

He'd rocked back out of reach with ease. "Before you start something I'll have to finish with a Taser, I suggest you have a cup of coffee. Then we can talk."

She pushed upright, setting her bare feet on the carpet. Her vision blurred, and dizziness swamped her.

Once the room stopped spinning, she said, "Whatever you gave me sure does pack a doozy of a hangover."

"Coffee." Standing up, he hiked his chin at a cup with a plastic lid on the nightstand. "Black, two sugars. Hope that's the way you still take it."

"I've cut out sugar." And carbs. The stuff was toxic and not doing wonders for her waistline. The older she got, the more closely she had to monitor what she consumed. Some women pulled off slim with little effort. She wasn't one of them.

"I'll remember that for next time," he said. "For now, a little sugar will make you feel better."

"Next time implies a future cordial exchange. There won't be one." She grabbed the coffee, flipped off the lid and took a sip. Letting out a low moan, she savored the next swallow of hot nirvana. Whether it was the effects of the drug or the fact that she'd given up sugar for the past six months, Kelly wasn't sure, but this was the best cup of coffee ever. "How do you see this playing out?"

"I was hoping for the easy way."

She chuckled. "Frankly, I think we're way beyond that, don't you?"

"Things could've been a lot harder in my perspective."

"Let me tase you, pump you full of an illegal psychoactive drug I picked up in a foreign country, dunk you in an ice bath and see how *easy* you think that is."

"Touché." He leaned against the far wall near the door, which was barricaded, and crossed his legs at the ankles. "For the record, I've apologized for that already."

He could take his apology and shove it where the sun didn't shine. "I don't know about easy, but this is pretty simple." She took another gulp of coffee. "Once I get my strength back, either I kill you or you kill me." Neither was a good choice, or one that she wanted. It was necessary.

Hunter and his team had to be eliminated. For the good of Langley. The country. So on and so forth.

His mouth quirked. "There is a third option."

She rolled her eyes. He wasn't naive and she wasn't gullible. There was no third option, but she'd play along. Stall. Sooner rather than later, someone at headquarters would wonder where she was, and then they'd send a team to find her.

"I'm listening," she said.

He pushed off the wall and edged forward. "Have you asked yourself why my team and I would risk our lives coming back here to Virginia just to speak with you when we could be halfway across the world?"

No. No, she hadn't. Her brain was still fuzzy, and last night she'd been preoccupied with other matters. Namely fighting and getting through a freezing-cold interrogation.

She glanced at the clock. Three thirty.

"I'll address the elephant in the room," he said. "I've got four, five hours tops to convince you of our innocence before the bloodhounds will be unleashed to find you."

If time was the elephant he was referring to, then there was a whole herd in the room. "Whether it's four hours or four hundred, you wouldn't be able to convince me. The best you could hope for at this point is to restrain me and run."

"We're done running." He took another step toward her, closing the gap between them. "Why would we come back here? What sense does that make unless we're innocent?"

His questions from last night replayed in her head. Each one had been about her possible guilt. Her setting them up. *Her* betrayal.

What game was he playing?

"Maybe you realized you can't win this," she said. "Not in the end. Sure, you made it off that island. Score one for the Topaz unit, but the CIA can't afford to lose this war. So, you're making a last-ditch effort to bring me over to your side. And if that's the case, it's quite desperate of you, not to mention futile."

"Someone set us up in Afghanistan to kill the wrong person. Our exit plan was blown, and we were attacked, but the team sent to take us out failed. Once we made our way back home, I texted you, arranged a meeting at the Tysons Corner Center. You confirmed, but instead of showing up, another kill team came in your stead."

That was the same story he'd spewed last night. But there had been no text from him. As far as she was aware, Hunter hadn't set foot in the United States again until now.

"You sent teams after Gage, Zee and Dean. They failed, too. Just like your two teams on the island."

Technically, Dean hadn't been a failure. In fact, he was the only success. The count was actually six to one in Topaz's favor.

"I'm not desperate," Hunter said. "Not yet. Trust me when I say you won't want it to come to that."

Desperate, out of options, cornered...that was precisely where she wanted them. "Really. Why not?"

"Because it means I have nothing else to lose, and then there won't be anything to stop me from burning Langley to the ground."

The idea of that was more chilling than the ice bath.

Bleary-eyed, she let her gaze travel over him, truly taking him in. Something she hadn't had a chance to do last night. His bearing was confident, bordering on cocky. Not in the least homicidal, which boded well for her. His golden-blond hair had grown out, but the shaggy look worked on him. Added to his rugged handsomeness. As did the tan. A collarless white pullover with sleeves pushed up to his forearms stretched across his muscular chest, and hip-hugging jeans encased his long legs. His physique was no less hardened by the months of frolicking on a Venezuelan beach. But his eyes were unreadable.

Why was he here? What could he possibly want from her?

"You've known me and my people a long time," he said, his voice growing softer as he held her gaze. "What we stand for. What's important to us."

"I thought I did." In spectacular fashion, they had proven her wrong. "After you went rogue, I had to re-examine everything. Question everything. Everyone."

For months, she'd been paranoid about traitors lurking around every corner. It was no way to live. She was burning the candle at both ends. Unable to sleep. Unable to decompress. In a constant state of suspicion and anxiety at home and at work.

If she still had a therapist, they'd have a field day with her.

"You need to ask yourself why we're here," Hunter said again. "What do we have to gain?" He let the question hang in the air before continuing. "There's only one reason all of us would come back here, in spite of what happened at Tysons eleven months ago. We're innocent. We thought you were the one responsible. That it had to be you since you were the only person who had access to everything. Not only the mission details but also our exit plan. But we didn't come for blind revenge. We came for the evidence we need to clear our names."

They could have killed her last night. There was no question of that, and right now they were expending precious hours on her, talking, when they should be running for their lives.

None of it added up.

She held the cup in both her hands, churning everything over in her mind. "If a kill team had come for you like you said, I assume gunfire was exchanged." The CIA were masters at cleaning up a scene, but Tysons Corner Center was a mega shopping mall. The place was massive, the largest in the metropolitan DC area. Always packed with civilians. In the age of smartphones, something would've been captured on video and aired on the news.

Nothing had been reported.

"There was a shoot-out," he said.

Shaking her head at his lie, she lowered her gaze and sighed.

He folded his arms across his chest. His biceps naturally flexed under his shirt, drawing her attention where it shouldn't be. "It was a Thursday at 10:00 a.m. Zee drove. She let us out in parking garage C. The rest of us entered from the southeast entrance and went to the third floor of Bloomingdale's. The shoot-out took place in the furniture department near the mattresses. The fire alarm had been pulled. It was the only reason civilians weren't injured. I'm sure the team got their dead out and that Langley wiped the security footage of the store."

"Of course they would've, and any cameras they missed are useless now. It's been almost a year. Stores only keep security videos for thirty days. Ninety, max. It's standard, as well you know. Conveniently makes it difficult to verify your story, doesn't it?"

He would have to try much harder than this to convince her.

"Let me show you what we have." He gestured to the small desk on the other side of the room.

A laptop was on the table, open, powered up and waiting.

She glanced back at Hunter. It wasn't as though she was able to take him in a fight, not yet, and access to the computer would give her a chance to send a distress email.

"All right," she said. "Show me." She stood, padded to the desk and sat in front of the computer.

"In the spirit of full disclosure, Zee made sure the laptop is air-gapped."

In layman's terms, the computer wasn't connected to the internet. So much for her chance to send an email.

Hunter put a hand on the back of the chair and leaned over beside her, looking at the laptop's screen.

She could feel him, the warmth from his body. She could smell him. No cologne. No aftershave. The scent was all his, and her belly tightened against it.

"Zee stayed in the vehicle. To be our eyes, she plugged into the live security feeds, monitoring things." He moved the mouse past several documents on the screen and clicked on an MP4 file. "She recorded it."

The video began as a montage of several feeds rolling at once. Various angles and positions in a mall. It looked as though it could've been Tysons. Then she noticed several stores that were only located at that particular mall in the area.

Date and time stamps lined up with what he'd told her. Although it was easy enough to doctor those.

"Footage can be altered," she said, staring at the recorded feeds.

"Just watch."

Hunter, Gage and Dean entered the mall. Not together. Staggered seconds apart. They were wearing ball caps, and their heads were lowered, faces turned away from the cameras. Still, she pinpointed them. The self-possessed swagger and their muscular builds gave them away. Also, she knew what to look for.

They made their way to Bloomingdale's, using different routes, and took up positions on the third floor.

The screens changed, showing a second team enter. Six men. Three from the southeast. Three more from the west. Same swagger. Similar body frames. No doubt mercenaries contracted for this purpose.

"It was at this point Zee gave us the heads-up about the other team."

"You would've had ample time to leave without engagement." She looked up at him. "Why didn't you?"

He turned his head and met her gaze, bringing his mouth dangerously close to hers.

Unwanted heat flooded her face, bled lower through her body.

"Because I was waiting for you," he said. "At first, I thought you were being cautious by having a team there as protection. Then this happened."

She turned back to the screen, grateful to break the up-close-and-personal eye contact.

One man approached Hunter in the furniture department. The guy waved, flashed a tentative smile, drew closer saying something.

"He knew our code word," Hunter said.

"Thermopylae?" The battle where a small force of Greeks made their last stand, despite overwhelming odds, and faced a vast Persian army. They'd decided on the phrase because if it was ever used, then it meant things were dire. An operative was out in the cold and might have to disappear or make a last stand.

Never had they thought the day would come when it would be needed. They were both pragmatists, long-range planners who didn't expect the world to end but wanted to be prepared in the event it did.

"How would he know, Kelly? Unless you had been the one to send him," Hunter asked.

Unease trickled down her spine as she stared at the footage.

The man drew first, holding a gun with an attached sound suppressor. He had Hunter in his sights, would've killed him if not for Gage.

The rest of the kill team had taken a prime position. Topaz was surrounded. The elevator was to their backs.

Muzzle flashes erupted from a different angle. Somewhere behind the mercenaries.

"Who helped you?" Kelly asked.

"Zee. Once she spotted the team, she parked closer to the store and made a beeline to our position."

On the video, Hunter and his men made it inside the elevator. Someone tossed a smoke grenade. Had to have been Zee.

White emergency lights began flashing.

The fire alarm must've been pulled.

Kelly racked her brain for every reason she shouldn't believe the veracity of the video. All the ways it could've been staged, altered, manipulated for effect.

"You don't want to believe what you've just seen," Hunter said. "Right now, you're running through a list of excuses not to. You've clung to the lie you were fed for so long, it's hard to accept anything else. But think about it. Furniture had been smashed. There were bullet holes in mattresses. Even if none of the employees witnessed what happened and the security footage is gone, the damage would've been reported. There also has to be a record of the fire department responding to the alarm."

Details so in the weeds someone might have forgotten to clean those up. No one would generally look that deep.

She turned toward him, their legs brushing as she looked at him. The contact was unexpected, brief, but enough to send a tingle through her. "Let's say I check it out and there is a security report. It would only prove something violent happened there on the day you specified. Not that you're innocent of murder for hire."

"It would also prove that we went there to meet someone. A friend. Instead, a kill team was sent. If not by you, then who?" Hunter lowered in front of her and knelt, putting himself in a physically vulnerable position.

She was aware he knew this, and he did it anyway.

Near her right hand on the desk was a ballpoint pen. A makeshift weapon within reach. This was her chance. The tip was sharp enough to puncture his throat if she used the right amount of force and provided her reflexes had recovered.

She could end this, here and now.

Using her middle finger, she rolled it slowly, discreetly into her palm. It was solid, heavy. One jab, maybe two, was all that it would take, but something stayed her hand.

To hurt an enemy in self-defense, to send a team of bloodthirsty mercenaries to handle the elimination, yes, she was capable of that.

To kill Hunter when he was pleading his case, staring her in the eyes, close enough to kiss…

She let the pen go and pressed her palm to the desk.

"Your father trusted me," he said, making anger spike through Kelly.

Her father had admired him, thought him to be a shining example of what was the best at headquarters. She'd been foolish enough to think the same. "You don't get to talk about him."

"You once trusted me, too," he added, putting a hand on her knee, and an old wound opened inside her. "After our mission, did you ever look into why someone would want to have Ashref Saleh murdered?"

He made it sound so ordinary, so small. As though they had taken out a low-level diplomat, someone inconsequential.

Ashref had been the deputy director of intelligence for Afghanistan, second in rank and power only to the president. Topaz had been sent to kill Khayr Faraj, a terrorist. Langley had intel that indicated Ashref was financing Khayr. If Topaz had caught him in the act, handing over a payment, then and only then had they been given authorization to eliminate Ashref. That could've been justified, explained. Hailed by the US and Afghanistan as a joint success.

In place of a triumph, Topaz had created a political quagmire that threatened to destabilize an ally.

"Of course we looked into why you did it." She shoved his hand from her leg.

His mouth compressed into a thin, hard line. "What answer did you come up with?"

"Ashref had struck a deal with the tribal leaders and farmers to reduce the number of opium poppy fields in exchange for government subsidies. The Taliban and warlords weren't happy about it, but they didn't want to eliminate Saleh themselves. It might have started a civil war. Instead, they paid you to kill him and a tribal leader who had rallied the farmers to support him."

He frowned. "I would never sell my honor and integrity. None of us were paid. We heard about the supposed offshore accounts in our names, but none of us have touched one red cent of that blood money."

Hunter was good. Truly. He almost had her.

Talk about convincing. He spoke with such conviction, like he believed this story. Either he was a pathological liar, or he was suffering a break from reality.

She snatched the pen and pressed the tip to his throat, right at the carotid artery. "Before they shipped me off to a black site, I was hauled into Price's office, where Andrew played a video for me."

Rather than defend himself, he leaned into the tip of the pen, daring her to give it a good, hard shove. "Of what?"

"*You.* Waltzing into the bank in the Cayman Islands. The very same day you withdrew two hundred and fifty thousand dollars. The video was also date and time stamped. You didn't even have the decency to hide your face from the camera."

Hunter recoiled as though he'd been physically hit. The man looked genuinely surprised. "I've never been to the Cayman Islands."

"I saw the video."

"It must have been fabricated. Real footage of me manipulated by whoever is behind this."

"But I'm supposed to believe without a shadow of

doubt that the video you showed me of Tysons Corner is real? Not manipulated in any way to produce a desired effect."

His jaw hardened.

They were at an impasse when it came to the videos. One of them had been doctored.

She'd believed in him once, accepted anything he told her. Those days were long gone.

Never again would she allow herself to be a fool.

"David Bertrand didn't think we were traitors," Hunter said, trying a different course of persuasion. "He knew something was awry with the mission and started digging around. That's why he was fired, went into hiding."

"What?" David had been an analyst assigned to Topaz in a support role back at Langley. He had worked on their last mission and had been privy to the details of the op and how it had all taken a turn for the worse. "No, he wasn't fired. He quit."

"Why do you think that?"

"After I was released from the black site and returned to Langley, I noticed he was gone and asked about him. An analyst told me he'd quit."

"Zee spoke to him minutes before David and his fiancée were murdered by the team you sent after Zee."

Kelly stiffened. David Bertrand was dead?

Whether he had been killed accidentally or specifically targeted, why hadn't she been briefed?

She sat back, lowering the pen. "Where did this happen?"

"In Idaho Falls."

Treat Yourself with 2 Free Books!

GET UP TO 4 FREE BOOKS & 2 FREE GIFTS WORTH OVER $20

See Inside For Details

Claim Them While You Can

Get ready to relax and indulge with your **FREE BOOKS** and more!

Claim up to FOUR NEW BOOKS & TWO MYSTERY GIFTS – absolutely FREE!

Dear Reader,

We both know life can be difficult at times. That's why it's important to treat yourself so you can relax and recharge once in a while.

And I'd like to help you do this by sending you this amazing offer of up to FOUR brand new full length FREE BOOKS that WE pay for.

This is everything I have ready to send to you right now:

Try **Harlequin® Romantic Suspense** books featuring heart-racing page-turners with unexpected plot twists and irresistible chemistry that will keep you guessing to the very end.

Try **Harlequin Intrigue® Larger-Print** books featuring action-packed stories that will keep you on the edge of your seat. Solve the crime and deliver justice at all costs.

Or **TRY BOTH!**

All we ask in return is that you answer 4 simple questions on the attached Treat Yourself survey. You'll get **Two Free Books** and **Two Mystery Gifts** from each series you try, *altogether worth over $20!* Who could pass up a deal like that?

Sincerely,

Pam Powers

Harlequin Reader Service

Treat Yourself to Free Books and Free Gifts.

Answer 4 fun questions and get rewarded.

	YES	NO
1. I LOVE reading a good book.		
2. I indulge and "treat" myself often.		
3. I love getting FREE things.		
4. Reading is one of my favorite activities.		

TREAT YOURSELF • Pick your 2 Free Books...

Yes! Please send me my Free Books from each series I select and Free Mystery Gifts. I understand that I am under no obligation to buy anything, as explained on the back of this card.

Which do you prefer?

❑ **Harlequin® Romantic Suspense** 240/340 HDL GRCZ
❑ **Harlequin Intrigue® Larger-Print** 199/399 HDL GRCZ
❑ **Try Both** 240/340 & 199/399 HDL GRDD

FIRST NAME

LAST NAME

ADDRESS

APT.#

CITY

STATE/PROV.

ZIP/POSTAL CODE

EMAIL ❑ Please check this box if you would like to receive newsletters and promotional emails from Harlequin Enterprises ULC and its affiliates. You can unsubscribe anytime.

HI/HRS-520-TY22

▶ DETACH AND MAIL CARD TODAY! ▶

© 2022 HARLEQUIN ENTERPRISES ULC
™ and ® are trademarks owned by Harlequin Enterprises ULC. Printed in the U.S.A.

HARLEQUIN Reader Service —Here's how it works:

BUSINESS REPLY MAIL
FIRST-CLASS MAIL   PERMIT NO. 717   BUFFALO, NY

POSTAGE WILL BE PAID BY ADDRESSEE

HARLEQUIN READER SERVICE
PO BOX 1341
BUFFALO NY 14240-8571

NO POSTAGE
NECESSARY
IF MAILED
IN THE
UNITED STATES

Kelly recalled mention of the location from the sit-rep about Zee. The clever hacker had evaded the kill team with the help of John Lowry.

Not one word regarding Bertrand had been in the report.

"David told Zee that he found discrepancies in files related to our mission, such as what Khayr Faraj looks like." There were no pictures of Khayr, only sketches based on a compilation of oral descriptions. "We were under the impression he had a birthmark shaped like an apple on his right cheek. David found a conflicting one that specified it was on his left cheek, not the right, and resembled a tree. Subtle discrepancies that led us to believe the tribal leader was Khayr."

A subtle disparity could make a world of difference. Something small would be easy to overlook, especially in the case of this operation. The mission had been assigned at the last minute. Top priority. From the very beginning, it had been rushed and no one had thought anything of it. When a high-value target like Khayr popped up on the radar, everyone scrambled to get them. Time was always of the essence. It was the nature of those types of assignments.

"What are you saying? Someone deliberately changed the mission details?" she speculated, struggling to think coolly.

"That's precisely what I'm saying."

If Topaz had been set up, then that would have been the best way to do it. Feed them misinformation that had them taking out the wrong target, all the while leading them to believe they were following orders, just doing their job.

"When David dug around after the mission," Hunter said, "he couldn't find any substantive intelligence that supported the claim Ashref Saleh was funding terrorism or financially backing Khayr. It was a lie."

"The whole mission was predicated on it. If Ashref had no illicit dealings with Khayr, the two of them wouldn't have had a reason to meet."

"And they didn't. That's why Khayr wasn't there. He was never supposed to be, because he wasn't the intended target. Ashref Saleh was."

Kelly's stomach did a long, sickening roll. David had been fired after finding discrepancies; he'd gone into hiding and was murdered, and she had been none the wiser.

"Everything we've found on Ashref shows that he was clean." Hunter knelt forward and opened a folder on the laptop. "Zee activated a zero-day virus in Langley's system that allowed her to retrieve these documents."

Kelly set the pen on the desk and looked through the files in the folder. Page after page added credence to his argument. She had to wonder if it was real. Had they manufactured this? With Zee's virus, did the hacker import these documents onto the CIA server to leave behind as supposed evidence?

It was possible.

"On every assignment," he said, "we always chose how to execute it. Except on this one. We were instructed to use explosives."

"That's not true. I remember the mission parameters. You were given the normal leeway to handle it as you saw fit."

"Did you brief us on that?" he asked.

"No. There wasn't time."

Things had moved at warp speed when they'd learned about the planned meeting between Ashref and Khayr. Every member of Topaz was highly experienced. They didn't require her oversight. At the time, she'd been managing a second team that was green and needed guidance on their first few missions. Her attention had been divided, but with Hunter leading his unit, she hadn't thought twice about it.

"Can you say without a doubt what parameters were specified on the classified laptop we were given?" Hunter asked. "Did you load it? Did you verify it? Or did you trust the system?"

The sickness in her stomach sneaked into her throat and tasted foul.

Hunter went on and on, marshaling the facts to support his claim that Topaz had been used and set up to assassinate Ashref. The more details he picked apart, the more on edge it put her.

Her brain felt broken, like it couldn't process all the facts. Perhaps due to the lingering effects of the drugs. Or perhaps it was because the tsunami of information put her on the wrong side of this war.

"Stop." She lifted her palm, needing a breather. They'd been going at this for hours, on an empty stomach, no less. "Give me a minute."

Getting up, she stretched her legs, sucked in a deep breath.

She went to the bathroom, ran the water, corralled her thoughts.

Plenty of things about his story rang true. Some details she would be able to verify on her own: a security report at the mall about damage on the day of the ambush, the fire department responding to the incident, whether David had been killed in Idaho Falls, the discrepancies in the mission.

The money in the offshore accounts could be explained as part of the scheme to incriminate the Topaz unit. Two million dollars sounded like a big number at first. Not so much when divided four ways. If they had been guilty, had been hired to kill Ashref, why wouldn't they simply come back home after the mission?

They could've claimed they thought the tribal leader had been Khayr. Mistakes happened.

As strange as it sounded, guilty people wouldn't have run. Not for five hundred thousand apiece. Dirty law enforcement kept playing the game, biding their time, building up their financial stash, eliminating those who knew the truth.

The certainty of it struck her full force.

Someone else at Langley was behind this. Someone dirty who wanted Topaz out of the picture, because they were innocent. Forced to run after being attacked on their way out of Afghanistan and once again at Tysons Corner.

But the surveillance footage of Hunter strolling into

the bank as casual as he pleased, smiling, no less, still bothered her.

It was the one piece of evidence that had cemented his guilt in her mind. After watching it, there was no way she was able to continue making excuses for them, and she had finally acknowledged them as traitors.

She looked in the mirror, past her haggard appearance, and stared into her eyes. "How stupid can you be?"

Whoever had done this knew that she'd believe the video. Knew she wouldn't question it. Knew it would sever the last threads of loyalty she had to Topaz.

Kelly splashed water on her face, patted her skin dry with a towel and left the bathroom.

Hunter stood, leaning against the desk with his arms crossed. The lethal glare of his eyes had her hesitating, told her something had changed. "If it wasn't you, *Red*, why were you promoted?"

A nervous thrill fluttered in her chest. Calling her the intimate nickname, after everything that had transpired, shouldn't affect her, but it did.

"I buy that you were interrogated at a black site." He stalked across the room. "But you didn't quit," he said, getting closer, lifting a hand and curling it around the side of her neck. "I'm having a tough time understanding why you were promoted if you weren't a part of this. Why would they reward you?"

"I told you. Price has been grooming me." She stepped back, trying to break his hold, but he wouldn't let go. In fact, he tightened his grip.

He dipped his head, bringing their faces as close as

possible without their noses touching, and captured her gaze. Disquiet and desire quivered in her belly in equal measures, her skin heating at his touch.

She hated the fact that he still had such a powerful effect on her. Threads of the deep, lingering attraction tugged at her, making her yearn to be even closer to him.

"After being the handler for a team that goes rogue," he growled, "after being interrogated, tortured, they promoted you over Andrew Clark, to the position of deputy director of operations. You don't think that's odd?"

"I've been working for this position most of my life. You know that. The long hours, the endless sacrifices. Price told me this was always meant for me. I almost lost it, but I proved my innocence at the black site." Hunter didn't understand the agony she'd suffered through for an endless week. The nightmare of it had messed with her head for months—it still tormented her. "The promotion was an early reward because of what I had endured."

His jaw grew tight as he studied her. "From where I'm standing, it looks like a bribe. Not a consolation prize." He let her go. "But tell yourself whatever you need to if it lets you sleep at night."

As he stepped back, she realized she was trembling from top to toe. From the proximity to him, but more so from his words. Each one she'd felt, and combined, they had alarm bells clanging in her head.

A bribe implied corruption at the very top.

Dr. Evil did exist, and his name was Wayne Price.

She drew in a long, steady breath, suppressing the rising sense of dread. "Let's say I'm willing to swallow the possibility that your team is indeed innocent. Then this wasn't about the Taliban and government subsidies. Why do you think Ashref was assassinated?"

This all boiled down to the *why.* Without that answer, they'd never find proof.

Hunter shrugged. "We need you to find the answer to that question."

Great.

"Hey, Red."

Her body strung tight, her thighs tingling, and she cursed the visceral reaction.

"My people and I have a lot at stake, and we're betting everything on you. Eight lives are in your hands. I've got to ask. Can I trust you to help us?"

She wanted to say yes.

She wanted to trust him.

She wanted him back in her life. Not as an enemy. As a friend. Hell, they'd been much more than that since Boston. She'd be a liar if she didn't admit that he was the only man she'd longed to have on a deeper level.

But years of wariness, the lingering burn of them going rogue, made it impossible for her to utter the word.

She wouldn't make him a promise that she wasn't certain she could keep. So, she told him the only honest thing she could. "You can trust me to find the truth. About all of it. Even my promotion."

"Thank you." He pulled her into a careful embrace, and she let him.

It seemed pointless to fight it. With his arms wrapped around her, he pressed his cheek to hers. His stubble brushed her face, and she was rubbed raw, not on her skin but deep inside.

The tenderness brought tears to her eyes, but she refused to cry and fall to pieces. Not when she had to steel herself to fight the real enemy.

No matter what it cost her, she wouldn't stop until she found the truth.

Chapter Nine

"You just let her go!" John said, getting in Hunter's face as though there had been a better choice.

"This wasn't something I did lightly. I weighed the decision carefully, factoring in the risks." Hunter kept his voice flat and moved around the room, looking at everyone else to prevent the conversation from escalating into a brawl. The only two not present were Kate and Olivia. With the likelihood of things getting heated, Zee didn't want her daughter in the room, and Kate had offered to keep her company. "Kelly agreed to wear a transmitter. We can see and hear everything she does."

His gut knotted at how badly this could backfire. He tried to defend himself mentally against John's rational arguments and common sense that agreed with the little voice in his head screaming this was a mistake.

"What good will that do us with the deputy director of the CIA?" John asked. "I take it she can't simply waltz into Langley wearing a device like that."

"No, she can't," Hunter admitted. "But there is a way around the sensors in the lobby. She'll have to remove it, temporarily, and hide the transmitter in the base of a specially lined travel mug that she has."

"When that happens," John said, "we'll be in the dark. The possibilities for Kelly Russell will become endless while we're exposed, with our possibilities shrinking by the minute."

It was true. Hunter wouldn't bother trying to deny it. This plan had holes, big gaping ones, but it was the best course of action. He hoped. "We all agreed that she's not the one who set us up," he pointed out.

"She didn't do it," Zee said, backing him up.

"If Hunter planted enough seeds of doubt about our guilt, then she'll help us," Dean chimed in.

"That's a mighty big *if.*" John shook his head with frustration written all over his face. "We don't know what's going through her head. There's nothing stopping her from standing by and allowing her team to kill us, if for no other reason than to make her life easier."

Putting their heads on proverbial spikes would simplify Kelly's life and ensure her position as deputy director, but she was better than that. Hunter was certain of it. She loved the CIA, being a part of something greater than herself, being of service to her country. Letting this conspiracy continue would go against everything she stood for.

"Integrity will stop her," Hunter said. In the end, she would do the right thing.

"Do the rest of you agree with his assessment?" John looked around the room. "Are you willing to bet your lives on it?"

Before they were divided on a decision that couldn't

be undone, Hunter turned to everyone. "I gave her a chance to take me out." He'd deliberately placed a ball-point pen next to the laptop. Heavyweight. Textured rubber grip. Stainless steel, with a sharp tip. A solid crude weapon in a pinch. Then he'd lowered to a knee, giving her the perfect angle to strike and succeed, even if she hadn't fully recovered. Gage had been on the other side of the motel room door, ready with the Taser in the event things went south. "But she didn't. Instead, she listened and asked the right questions."

"Can you look me in the eye and tell me she's one hundred percent Team Topaz?" John asked.

"No, I can't." Hunter shook his head, and John gave a heavy sigh. "But she is on the side of the truth. She'll find out who is responsible. Of that, I have no doubt."

"Forgive me if I don't share in your confidence," John said. "We can't stay here. This location is com-promised."

"I agree." Hunter looked at Zee. "Has everything already been arranged?"

"Yes," she said. "I've booked new rooms in a place similar to this but near Bailey's Crossroads."

That was much closer to Arlington, Alexandria and McLean than their current position. There would be an uptick in CCTV coverage around the new location. They'd have to take additional precautions.

"The rest of you will relocate," Hunter said. "I'll stay here and monitor the surveillance feed. That way when I meet with her again, I won't expose you all."

"John made valid points," Dean said. "When Kelly

comes back here, she might not be alone. It'll be a tough spot for you to get out of on your own."

"I can hang back." Gage stepped out of the corner where he'd been monitoring the surveillance feed on Kelly, and Hope's eyes flared wide with alarm. "If she brings Quinlan and the others—"

"I'll handle it," Hunter said. "Alone."

"This isn't a smart move," Zee said. "Let one of us stay."

"It's not up for debate." He was grateful they were willing to have his back on this, even if it cost them. "Get moving. I'll check in regularly with updates."

This would work. It had to. He was betting on Kelly and that she would come through. In the event he was wrong, no one else should have to suffer for his error in judgment. They all had others who loved them, needed them to survive this.

If Kelly betrayed him, he would be the only one to pay the price.

KELLY HURRIED DOWN the hall at Langley, headed toward the operations room.

After Hunter had dropped her off at home, she'd grabbed her go bag, which was packed with essentials, and quickly changed her clothes while keeping on the pendant necklace with hidden camera and audio. The only time she'd taken it off was to get it through the lobby undetected.

Getting caught wearing the device would be considered treasonous, but she understood the necessity from Hunter's perspective. He was trusting her, once again, with the lives of his entire team. His level of faith in her only bolstered her growing fears that the Topaz unit had been unjustly persecuted.

The CIA had been their judge, jury and would-be executioner.

She was appalled by her part in it. By how she had allowed someone in these hallowed halls to play her for a fool.

Kelly pushed through the tinted door of the operations room and stopped cold.

"How nice of you to finally join us," Andrew said.

"What are you doing here?" she asked, swallowing the profanity she'd wanted to use.

"Your job, apparently, since you were missing in action." The corner of his mouth hitched up. "There's been a development. The analysts have been trying to reach you, to no avail."

"I was indisposed." Both of her cell phones were dead when she got home. She'd charged them in the car and had been in such a rush she hadn't checked the messages. "That doesn't explain your presence in my ops room, much less the building."

Andrew was still staring at her with a hint of a smirk. "I stopped in to make sure I didn't leave anything outstanding and to check that ops were fully covered before I started my vacation. It's a good thing I was here."

"You just happened to stop in?" She regretted the question as soon as it left her lips. They both knew he hadn't. She wouldn't be surprised if he'd never left the building and had slept in his office. He was a cautionary case of what not to become. "Is Price aware you're here?"

"When I updated him, he was the one who said I was, and I quote, *invaluable*." The smirk turned to a full-blown smug smile now. Patronizing. "He sees now how much I'm needed."

She swallowed the nasty retort building on her tongue, not wanting to sling mud with him in front of the analysts. The man was teeth-grindingly aggravating. "What's the urgent development?"

"We have reason to believe the entire Topaz unit is here. In Virginia."

A chill ran through Kelly, like someone had walked over her grave. "Based on what?" she asked, keeping her voice level and her face deadpan.

"Show her," Andrew said to Ebony.

The lead analyst hit a few keys, changing one of the displays on the wall of monitors at the front of the room. An image of Gage came up.

"How did we get this?" Kelly asked.

"Pure luck." Andrew clucked his tongue.

"We haven't had any hits on CCTV, not even from passive surveillance like security cameras on ATMs or traffic cams," Ebony said. "This photo of Gage Graham is actually in the background of the main photo. It's been zoomed in and enhanced. Two women were taking a selfie and caught Graham behind them in a parking lot. Our facial recognition program got a ping after they posted the pictures on Facebook and Snapchat. We pinpointed the location to a big-box store that's only twenty minutes away."

Hunter was monitoring the live feed from the necklace. He would take appropriate action to ensure his people stayed safe. At least that was one thing Kelly didn't have to worry about.

"If one of them is here in the local area," Andrew said, "I think it's safe to assume they all are, but I haven't been able to figure out why. I contacted your attack dog, Quinlan. Beta team is all over this." Andrew turned to her. "What's wrong with you? Why don't you look thrilled?"

"I am." Kelly tore her gaze from the monitors and looked at him. "This is great news."

"This is still your op." Andrew shoved his hands in his pockets. "Price made that clear. But I'll stick around and help you cover down on this. A lot of moving parts. Figured you'd need an extra hand, so we don't miss anything."

She could use this to her advantage. "That's fine."

Andrew narrowed his eyes. "Really? You're not going to give me any pushback on this after yesterday?"

"I'm a professional. Not a territorial animal incapable of rational thought and civility. Besides, I know this mission means as much to you as it does me."

"That it does. Topaz went rogue on both of us."

"Since you've already got things under control, why don't you run the op today?" Handing over the reins to Andrew would free her up to dig around in Topaz's last mission.

He hesitated a moment. "What's the catch?"

"Absolutely none. If this fails, I'll still take full responsibility."

Giving a slow nod, he didn't hide the suspicion from his face. "Okay."

Kelly turned to leave, but when she reached the door, she stopped. "Out of curiosity, whatever happened to David Bertrand?"

"David?" He walked up to her, drawing close enough for her to smell his cheap aftershave mingled with sweat. "He quit."

"Did he give his resignation to you?"

He edged even closer and lowered his voice. "I was at the black site with you when he decided to leave." His stale-coffee breath fanned her face, and her stomach turned. "One of the analysts updated me. Why?"

She took a step back. "He was so good at his job, it would be nice to have someone like him working on this, too. Never hurts to have too much brainpower. Be sure to brief me on any updates."

Eyeing her warily, he nodded. "I will."

Kelly shoved through the door and hurried down the maze of corridors to her office. At seeing Price's door closed, she let out a small breath of relief. She didn't want more questions about her whereabouts earlier this morning slowing her down.

"Good morning, Ms. Russell." Her executive assistant, Steve, smiled. "Can I get you coffee?"

Another wave of nausea rolled through her stomach. "No, thanks. I'm fine. Unless there's something urgent, I don't want to be disturbed for any reason before lunch."

"Understood," Steve said, flashing a pleasant smile. He was one of the most efficient assistants at Langley, and with the flip of an internal switch he could become the ultimate sentinel.

Closing the door to her office, she took off her overcoat and hung it up. She slipped into her chair behind her desk, shoved her ID into the smart card reader and booted up her computer. Looking around her office, she noticed, perhaps for the first time, what everyone else must see when they walked in. The space could belong to anyone. There was nothing personal to mark it as hers. No photos. No unique artwork. Not a shred of sentiment. The room was as cold and sterile as her life.

At home, she had a few pictures of her parents and godmother on the mantel above the fireplace. Still, none with friends, on vacation, celebrating a major life event. She even kept her trophies from martial arts tournaments boxed up in the garage.

Turning to the computer, she logged on, entering her lengthy password, and opened a bottle of water while she waited for system authentication. Finally, she was in. Another password to access the most restricted database. Red banners on all sides of the screen highlighted words denoting different compartments, additional levels of classification. She clicked past a series of screens acknowledging the sensitivity of the information. Accepting the consequences of disclosure—going to jail for a very long time.

This endeavor was a gamble. A big one. Provided she learned anything, she'd have to share it with Hunter, which would only drag her into this deeper.

There was a sinking feeling in her chest, but she'd

made a vow, not only to Hunter, but also to herself. She needed the truth.

In the search engine, she entered two keywords: *Ashref Saleh*.

Links to a multitude of files popped up on the screen. A combination of data ranging from the low side to the highest possible classification.

She scrolled past anything labeled *unclassified, confidential* or *secret*. Everyone in the building with access to a computer had clearance to read those files.

Instead, she focused on the top-secret documents that were labeled with an additional code word based on sensitivity. She tapped on a file, opening it.

She gave it more than a cursory glance, zipping over every word. Five pages of information she already knew, confirming Ashref's efforts to thwart the opium industry in Afghanistan with subsidies to farmers.

The next two were more of the same. Nothing on a connection to him and terrorism or Khayr Faraj. What if it didn't exist?

One link at the bottom of the screen had a code word for a highly classified electronic surveillance program. The intelligence community had several running at the moment, but this file could only be accessed by a handful of people at Langley. Not even David Bertrand would've been able to get to it.

She moved the cursor and clicked the link.

The document opened, and what she saw set her nerves on fire.

It was redacted.

Two pages. Ninety percent of the lines had been

blacked out. At her current clearance level, she had access to everything the president was briefed on. Nothing was redacted. Until now.

This was it.

In her gut, she knew that whatever was in this document was the reason Ashref had been killed.

All she could make out was his name, that he had been talking to someone about something, and it'd been deemed a "grave threat to US national security."

If Khayr Faraj had been mentioned, there was no way for her to tell for certain, but she doubted it. Keeping the terrorist's name visible would've supported the reason for Topaz's last op, and anyone who saw this would draw the natural conclusion.

This redaction was to cover up the truth.

She kicked herself mentally for never going through any of the files before, for not searching for hard evidence of her own.

Everything had happened in a whirlwind. The mission had gone awry, and the team had disappeared. Her biggest fear was that they had been killed. A flurry of reporting had come out about Ashref and the tribal leader. As they'd scrambled to piece together what had happened, news came in that the pilot who was supposed to transport Topaz out of Afghanistan was dead.

Still not a word from Hunter, or so she had thought.

Then the money in the offshore accounts had been discovered. Two days later, she was watching the video of Hunter going into the bank in the Cayman Islands. Before she had a chance to investigate, they'd hauled her off to that black site.

After the weeklong interrogation, the torture, she'd been so grateful, to be alive, not to be implicated with a team of suspected traitors, to have her reputation intact, to be rewarded with a promotion.

In the aftermath, she didn't want to think about any of it. She had wanted to forget and move on.

But all this time, she'd been stuck.

Voices outside her door pulled her from her thoughts. Steve and another man. Not Andrew.

Director Wayne Price.

Without a knock, the door swung open. Price strolled in with Steve on his heels.

"I'm sorry," Steve said to her, "I tried to explain you were busy."

"Leave us." Price shooed him out of the office and shut the door in his face.

Kelly closed the file and screen locked the computer. "To what do I owe the pleasure of you coming across to my side of the hall?" Something he had never done. She'd always been summoned.

Price walked to the large window that provided a view of the Potomac River in the distance. He clasped his hands behind his back and gazed outside. "Your predecessor, Matt, was brilliant, a workaholic, perceptive and stubborn as a mule. In many respects, you're very much like him. After three years of working seventy-hour weeks, he finally took a vacation with his family. To a ski resort in Vermont. His wife told him not to go down this one treacherous trail on the mountain. The Beast. There were signs posted about the dangers. Warnings that it was for the most advanced skiers only.

But Matt insisted he had to do it. Wouldn't listen. He might've made it, too, but there was an avalanche. You know, they never did find his body."

Kelly's throat tightened as she stiffened in her chair. She considered saying something but thought better of it. The accident had happened not long after Topaz's mission.

She recalled someone had told her in passing how avalanches in Vermont were as uncommon as getting the measles.

But she hadn't paid it much attention. Everyone had chalked up the accident to bad luck. Shortly after, she'd been promoted.

Price turned around, fixing her with his gaze. "Matt had the potential to lead this agency one day. He would've achieved great things, too. If only he'd recognized the danger. Heeded the warnings."

Kelly fiddled with her father's ring, twisting it around her finger.

Price crossed the room slowly, as though he had all the time in the world, sat on the edge of her desk beside her chair and put a hand on her shoulder. "Some things are better left alone." He glanced at her computer screen and looked back at her. "A curiosity you don't dare indulge. Because like the Beast, it can get you killed." His pointed words sent a chill through her. "You have the potential to succeed me, to run the CIA one day, to achieve great things. I want that for you. Truly." He patted her shoulder, giving a soft smile that made her skin crawl. "We all need to know when to submit to greater forces and choose a different course of action in the interest of self-preservation."

He was threatening her. A veiled but nonetheless clear threat.

The sensitive files about Ashref were flagged. Once opened, Price must receive a notification about who accessed them. That was how he'd known David Bertrand had been digging around.

Kelly cleared her throat and shifted in her chair so that his hand fell from her shoulder. "Since Andrew is here, overseeing Operation Cujo, I think I'll take those couple of days off that you offered him."

Surprise flickered across his features. "That sounds marvelous." Eyes brightening, he nodded his head emphatically. "Yes, absolutely. Get out of the office. Take your mind off this horrible business with Topaz. Let us handle it. I would've suggested a little downtime, but you can be so stubborn."

"As a mule." She pulled on a forced smile. "But I understand your words of wisdom." Advice that her conscience wouldn't allow her to heed.

"I'm relieved to hear it." He stood and walked to the door. "I'll let Andrew know. We won't bother you unless it's to notify you that the situation has been resolved."

Resolved. What a placid way of saying that a team had been slaughtered.

She tightened her smile and turned to her computer. "I'm logging off as we speak."

There was little point in sticking around. One call to the IT department, and he would be able to monitor everything she accessed.

Kelly pulled her ID from the card reader and grabbed her coat.

Price opened the door, and they headed out together.

"I'm taking a couple of days off," she said to Steve.

His jaw dropped. "What? Why? Are you sick?"

The questions were partly out of concern for her, but mostly for himself. "No, I'm not contagious or anything. You can relax."

Steve sagged with relief. "Good to know. Enjoy your time."

Price walked her to the hall that ran between their office suites. "It's a prudent decision to take care of yourself. I would hate for anything to happen to you," he said. Then, as though it was an afterthought, he added, "From the stress of overworking. It can be a hazard to your health."

"I would hate that, too." She might not be able to find what she was looking for at Langley, but there was someplace else she could get answers.

She was nothing if not resourceful.

With a curt wave, she turned and hustled down the hall. A little maze of turns took her to the elevators. She'd wait to remove the necklace in the lobby bathroom before she got near the sensors. The need to get out of there as quickly as possible pushed in on her.

She hit the call button, strategizing her next stop. The ODNI—Office of the Director of National Intelligence—was a closer drive, but her presence there would raise all sorts of alarm bells, and Price would get a phone call ten minutes after she set foot inside the building.

The elevator dinged. The doors opened. She hopped

inside the empty car and hit the button for the lobby. The doors started to close, but someone shoved an arm between them, engaging the safety sensor and forcing them to open.

Ebony got on and hit the button for the second floor. Once the elevator slipped into motion, she met Kelly's gaze in the reflection of the doors. "I heard what you said about David Bertrand."

The comment about wishing he were on the team. It had only been a cover to keep Andrew from getting suspicious. She hadn't meant to offend anyone. "You're a top-notch analyst. I wouldn't have anyone else leading the team."

"I know. My ego isn't fragile as eggshells."

Grinning, Kelly turned to her.

"Don't look at me. In case they're watching," Ebony said. The surveillance of the elevators didn't have audio, only video. "David didn't quit. He was fired. Security escorted him out the day they sacked him."

Her desk had been next to his, separated by a cubicle wall panel. Of course some of the other senior analysts must've witnessed what had happened.

"This past December," Ebony continued, "they killed him."

Kelly washed all expression from her face. "How do you know he's dead?"

"I was the support analyst assigned to the team that was sent after Zenobia. A kill order came in on David one night. It was in the same location where they had tracked Zenobia. According to protocol, I passed it along to the team leader."

"Where was this?"

"Idaho Falls."

Just as Hunter had told her. He'd been telling the truth about everything, and she'd doubted him, had sent two hit squads after him. Her actions filled her with shame. "Who initiated the kill order on David?"

"I don't know."

Damn.

But it must've been Price. He might have been able to get the order through without her knowledge, but every analyst's report on anything Topaz-related made it to her desk. She remembered this one, and there'd been no mention of David.

"Why didn't you include this information in your situation report?" Kelly asked.

"That's just it. I did." The elevator chimed. "Once it was completed, I sent the report to Clark for review." The doors opened. Ebony stepped off, and without looking back she said, "David deserves justice."

David Bertrand, the pilot in Afghanistan, Ashref Saleh, the tribal leader who had died alongside him and every member of Topaz deserved justice.

Kelly was going to do everything in her power to make that happen.

Chapter Ten

At the front desk of the National Security Agency head-quarters, Kelly signed in. Langley had an impressive campus sitting at 258 acres. The NSA dwarfed CIA headquarters in comparison. The behemoth agency occupied one and a half times as much land on Fort Meade in Maryland.

A guard passed her a visitor's badge, and she clipped it to the lapel of her suit jacket. Once he cleared her through the security checkpoint, she spotted Zach.

Tall and lean, he strode toward her wearing a suit with a slim cut and an impeccable fit. A light salmon-colored shirt flattered the olive tones of his skin. His thick black hair was brushed back, not a strand out of place.

"I hope you didn't come out on my account." Kelly gave him a quick one-armed embrace before he had a chance to wrap her into one of his bear hugs.

He'd always had a thing for her and had been the first boy to kiss her when they'd both been teenagers. Immediately afterward she knew she'd never see him as anything more than a brother.

"They always notify Public Affairs when a bigwig such as yourself," he said, waggling his eyebrows, "pops in unexpectedly." He walked her to the bank of elevators, hit the call button, and the doors opened. "What brings you by?"

They stepped inside together. Kelly hit the button for the top floor.

"I need to see Judith to get some information."

"Anything I can help you with?"

"I wish, but I need an analyst." Someone with complete access at the highest levels who could comb through a mountain of information quickly.

"Don't you have a legion of those at your command at Langley?"

"I do, but it's complicated."

The ride up was smooth, and he got off with her, sticking to her side.

"I'm going to hit the restroom first. It was great to see you."

"Oh, I'll wait for you."

Smothering a groan, she entered the ladies' room and ducked into a stall.

IN KEEPING WITH the agreement that she'd made with Hunter, she pulled the insulated thermos from her handbag—it was a large leather tote that held everything but the kitchen sink—and retrieved the surveillance necklace hidden in a compartment in the base.

Quickly, she put it on, hooking the clasp. She held up the pendant to her face. "As promised." It was the least she could do, even though it was like putting a Band-Aid on a gunshot wound.

She wished she'd had a phone number so she could speak with Hunter. To discuss everything. To apologize. To beg his forgiveness for falling into the designated role of adversary when he'd needed her. If she could go back in time, she'd make different choices. Starting with the morning after in the hotel room in Boston. To do it over again and confess how she'd felt about him.

If only she hadn't been such a coward, they might have figured out how to be in a relationship given their jobs and found a way to be together.

Although she didn't have his number, she was willing to bet that he had hers. But he hadn't called her on the long car ride from McLean, Virginia. Probably for operational security. It was safer to stay off the phones, especially one the CIA could hack and eavesdrop on.

Kelly stowed the travel mug in her bag and left the bathroom.

The security guard had already notified her godmother, Judith Farren, that she was on her way up. Kelly didn't want to keep her waiting. Judith always had a jam-packed schedule and was willing to give her two minutes. She couldn't afford to squander the opportunity.

In the hall, Zach stood patiently. He flashed a bright white smile worthy of a toothpaste commercial at her, and she couldn't help smiling back. Zach was like a breath of fresh air—in small doses.

"I really don't need an escort," she said.

"It's no trouble. Not where you're concerned."

He offered his arm, and she took it as they walked down the hall.

Judith's assistant greeted them and waved her into the office.

Her godmother was already on her feet behind her desk, gathering some folders and a notepad. With a smile, she held out a single arm in welcome. "How lovely of you to drop by, my dear." They gave each other air kisses, a custom they had in public since Judith was meticulous about her makeup. "I haven't seen you since Christmas. Far too long."

A pang of guilt sliced through Kelly. She only reached out to Judith when she needed something, and that wasn't often. Not because she didn't love her or enjoy her company—on the contrary. They were both compulsive workers, addicted to the grind. Or perhaps the emptiness in their lives made them cling tighter to their jobs.

"I've been meaning to get together to do lunch," Kelly said, glancing at Zach, who stood silent and observant like a fly on the wall.

"You picked a hectic day for a visit, but I trust you didn't drive to Maryland for a social call." Judith stayed in motion as always, only pausing in front of a mirror long enough to tuck a loose strand of hair in her chignon and check her teeth. Then she was headed for the door. "Walk with me. I have a meeting I can't skip. Sorry."

"No need to apologize. I'm the one who showed up unannounced."

"What can I do for you?"

There were others in the hall, also in a hurry. Although Judith had a presence that couldn't be ignored, no one seemed to be paying any attention to their conversation. Other than Zach, who traipsed alongside them.

Still, precaution never got anyone killed. "I need information that I can't get at home," she said, assured Judith would understand that she meant Langley.

"Problems with Father?" Judith asked.

"Let's just say I've been denied full access."

"You think you can find what you need in my house?"

"Yes." Without a doubt. It was related to a surveillance program. What the NSA didn't have control over, they had full knowledge of.

Judith stopped outside a conference room door. "Care to share with me?"

"I'd rather not." Kelly put a hand on her forearm. "I don't want to get you involved any more than I have to. Father is on the warpath."

Judith studied her with concern. "Are you safe?" The words, filled with alarm, snagged Zach's attention, bringing him to Kelly's side.

She looked between mother and son. "I can handle myself."

"It better stay that way. I had to bury Elliot," Judith said, referring to Kelly's real father. "I won't bury you, too. A parent should never have to go through that. I may not be your mother, but I love you like my own."

Kelly's mother had passed away when she was too young to remember her. Judith had stepped up, filling in the role as best she could. In so many ways, Kelly emulated Judith as the one female role model she admired. Everything she knew about how to dress, do her makeup, wear her hair in a professional environment, carry herself, she'd learned from Judith.

Zach put an arm around Kelly. "We both love you."

She wondered in what form his love came—familial or romantic. She could never shake the vibe that it was the latter.

"I'll be fine." Kelly stepped out from under his partial embrace. "It's nothing for either of you to worry about." In her experience, downplaying the severity of the matter was better than getting Judith worked up.

The conference door opened, and one of Judith's aides stuck his head out. "There you are. The general is ready to get started."

"I'll be there in a moment," Judith said easily, never one to get flustered. When the aide disappeared back inside the conference room, Judith turned to her. "You want to put one of my analysts in the crosshairs of whatever tiff you're having at home?"

"I'll do what I can to protect them. I only need them to do research. Nothing more."

Judith nodded. "Pick whoever you want. Tell them I give permission for them to clear their plate of everything else until they get you what you need. If you have any hiccups, let me know."

Kelly smiled. It was nice to have powerful people she could rely on. "Thank you."

"Do you need a list of analysts to consider? I can have my assistant give you some names."

"That won't be necessary." She had worked closely

with the NSA for years and had made it her business to form a rapport with a few of the analysts, but there was one in particular she had a long history with. "I already have someone in mind."

"I'll take you over to Analysis," Zach offered.

"That won't be necessary. I'd rather go on my own." Kelly patted his forearm.

"Zach, I'm sure you have a full plate," his mother said, understanding Kelly didn't want him hovering. "If you don't, then we're paying you far too much."

"I was only trying to be helpful. I'll go back downstairs to my cubbyhole in Public Affairs."

Kelly kissed his cheek, relieved to be rid of him.

SEATED IN A small, private conference room next to Kelly, Freddie Herschel rubbed his forehead. His pale face was taut with worry, twisting his features. "Why couldn't you have told me all this outside? Now I need a cigarette."

Kelly crossed her legs and sat back in the ergonomic chair. "Smoking can kill you."

"Apparently, so can this fact-finding mission you want me to undertake. I can't believe they killed David Bertrand over this. Why did you come to me?"

Freddie was wearing a long-sleeved T-shirt with the Starfleet insignia designed out of smaller pictures of different starships and the slogan 100% TREKKIE written across the top, which suited him perfectly. He looked like a combination of geek and the friendly guy next door. The man you asked to house-sit or translate a message written in Vulcan.

"I trust you," she said. "Implicitly. You're one of the good ones." She was taking a huge chance by sharing details with him, but he needed to understand what was at stake and the risks of getting involved. The last thing she would do was drag someone into this completely blind.

"It doesn't pay to be a nice person. David was a good one, and look where that got him."

She agreed, but saying so wouldn't encourage him to help. "All I need you to do is find out which surveillance program is tied to Ashref Saleh. The redacted document I saw was dated thirteen months ago."

"Well, that's easy enough. We only use Arcane and Silent Shadow in Afghanistan."

The Arcane program was eavesdropping at its finest. Only on allies. Everything from phone conversations to internet activity on worldwide providers based in the US, such as Google, Facebook, Microsoft. Data gathered included emails, videos, photos, even file transfers.

Silent Shadow involved intercepting routers, servers and other network hardware being shipped to targeted organizations in foreign countries. Covert firmware was installed before they were delivered.

Both programs were vital to the continued success of CIA operations overseas. If Ashref found out about either, it would be a motive.

"I need to know which one and exactly what made Ashref Saleh a threat to Langley. Anything you dig up on him and the program, print it out and get it to me." Speculation wasn't going to cut it. She needed documentation clearly connecting the dots.

"Whoa. Hang on a minute." Freddie raised his palms. "You never said anything about wanting me to become the next Snowden."

"That's a gross exaggeration of what I'm asking."

"The guy printed out classified documents, stuffed them in his pants and smuggled them out of NSA headquarters so that he could go public with the information."

Okay, phrasing it that way did make it sound exactly like what she was asking him to do. Ninety-nine percent of the computers at the NSA didn't have a USB port, to prevent someone from downloading classified information on a flash drive. Printing the documents and sneaking them out was the only way. "This isn't to betray your country, and I don't plan to go public."

"Then how are you going to clear the Topaz unit?"

She hadn't gotten that far in the plan. Her priority was getting the rest of the pieces to the puzzle. "There are smarter, better courses of action than going to the press. I suspect the documentation I'm asking you to get will provide a clear motive. That, combined with other evidence that I have, will be enough for the director of national intelligence to exonerate the Topaz unit." The DNI guided the entire intelligence community. To ensure nothing got swept under the rug, she would insist that the secretary of defense be in the loop on everything.

"Where did you get this other evidence if you're locked out at Langley?"

The evidence was Hunter's, but she didn't want Freddie to know that she was in contact with him. Not yet.

After she got her hands on the NSA documentation, she'd be willing to share more. "From a friend, but their hands are tied at this point. I need you."

Freddie lowered his gaze to his lap. "The DNI will have to conduct an independent investigation for verification before taking action. In the time that takes, I could be exposed. Someone could make me disappear."

"The independent investigation would only be a formality. To make things official. It would be done quickly and quietly due to the sensitive nature of the circumstances. You could take a well-timed leave of absence."

"I don't know." Freddie rubbed the bald spot at the top of his head. "Did Director Farren give authorization for me to smuggle out documents?"

"I don't want to make her complicit in this part." She didn't want to open her godmother up to the possibility of reprisals. Judith had worked too hard for too long to become the first female director of the NSA. Kelly wouldn't ruin such a remarkable achievement for her. Judith would have a far-reaching impact for years to come.

"Do you know how risky this is? What if I get stopped and searched on my way out of the building? What am I supposed to do if I get caught? This is my career, my life we're talking about."

"Not just yours. There are eight others with everything on the line. Ten if you include me." She was all in and had already crossed the point of no return. This was do or die.

"You're asking a lot from me," Freddie said. "I'm

no hero. I'm not a risk taker. I don't even bluff when I play poker."

"Real heroes are ordinary citizens who decide to do what's right even though they're afraid." Despite her fearless facade, this conspiracy terrified her. But turning a blind eye wasn't an option. She waited to give Freddie a chance to think. The tension between them swelled, and when he didn't seem swayed, she said, "You could always log me in to a computer and walk away. Let me do it."

She owed Hunter more than she could ever repay. Regrets were worthless. Nothing short of full exposure of the truth and Topaz exonerated would suffice. And she was willing to do whatever was necessary to make it happen.

"As if," Freddie scoffed. "When this all comes out, it'll look ten times worse on me if I let someone else use a computer under my log-in."

Asking another analyst for assistance increased the likelihood of Price finding out about this gamble. Freddie was the only one she completely trusted not to spill his guts and to actually follow through. "If you don't help me, think about what will happen to the Topaz unit. Hunter, Gage, Zee, Dean. They have civilians with them." Freddie had met some of the operatives. Intel was a small world. Playing on the fact that he could put faces to names felt dirty but necessary. "Zee's daughter is caught up in this. She's only eleven."

Freddie tipped his head back and sighed. "Using the kiddie card is so unfair."

It was, and she was sorry for it. "Defending our nation. Securing our future." That was the NSA's motto. Words Freddie took to heart.

For a long moment, he said nothing, his gaze roaming around the room, then he nodded. "All right. No more twisting my arm behind my back. I'm your man."

"Thank you. How long do you think it'll take you?"

He shrugged. "It depends on how many systems I need to access. Maybe a few hours. You want me to be thorough, find absolutely every thread that could be a motive, right?"

"Yes, of course." Exactly what she needed. "Can you do it discreetly without accessing any files that are shared with Langley?"

"I don't know. I'll sure try."

"If you do access shared files, don't go home. I'll rent a room for you at a hotel in cash, untraceable."

Freddie grimaced like he was having second thoughts. "What'll happen to Coco?"

She wasn't aware he had a girlfriend, not that she knew a lot about his personal life. It was another reason she had chosen him. No immediate family to endanger, or so she had thought. "Who is she? Do you live together?"

"She's my cat."

Kelly suppressed a smile. "The hotel would just be a precaution in the event you open shared files. If it comes down that, I promise your cat will be cared for. Maybe even get you a room that will allow small pets." She wrote down her cell number for him. "Don't use any related keywords over the phone in case my line is being monitored. We'll meet in person once you have something. Give a place and time. Also, use a code word if you found pay dirt, something concrete."

"What about 'avocado'?"

Kelly frowned. The word was a solid choice, unrelated to the subject matter. It had simply taken her by surprise.

"I love avocados," he said. "I eat them every day."

"Okay. On the flip side, if its inconclusive, say something like—"

"Okra." Smiling, he pushed his glasses up the bridge of his nose. "I can't stand it."

"Are you sure you haven't done this before? You're a natural." She patted his hand. "Don't say anything else on the phone. Not even your name."

Freddie nodded again, clearly uncertain about the task ahead of him. "When I contact you, don't be late. If you're not there at the specified time, I'll leave and shred whatever I have. I'm not hanging around anywhere with classified documents. I mean it."

Based on the look in his eye, she could tell he was serious. "Fair enough, and this should go without saying, but don't trust anyone else on this."

"Got it. I won't." Freddie stood to leave.

"One more thing. Be careful."

HUNTER HIT A button on the laptop, stopping the recording from the surveillance necklace, and opened the motel door before Kelly had a chance to knock. His heart jumped at the sight of her. When she stepped across the threshold, she wasn't the deputy director of operations. She wasn't the enemy he had to recruit.

Right then, she was the woman who had put the welfare and future of his team above herself and her own ambition.

"Sorry it took me so long to get back." She removed her coat. "I wanted to make sure I wasn't followed. I didn't want to risk leading anyone back here to the entire team."

It had taken her three hours since she'd left Fort Meade. She was thorough, he'd give her that.

He locked the door and watched her dump her bag in a chair and kick off her shoes while he glanced over the long, sexy muscles running the length of her slender body.

"I'm also sorry for doubting you," she said. "I do know you. Who you are at your core, and I should've trusted in that." Averting her gaze, she lowered her head, and he imagined how difficult this must be for her. "I'm so ashamed for my part in this. For the way I led the hunt on you all. Can you forgive me, for letting you down, for not being there when you and your team needed me most?"

"After everything you went through, your actions are understandable."

"You didn't answer my question."

He brushed the back of his hand across her cheek, along her jaw and tipped her chin up with a knuckle, meeting her tortured gaze. "I can forgive you anything." The words spilled from his mouth without him thinking, but he realized they were true.

For a second, those agonizing moments, forced to go into hiding, running for his life, trying to survive on the island, Kelly in the crosshairs of his sniper rifle, the interrogation he'd subjected her to, the anger... It all evaporated.

The past tangled with the present as heat speared through him.

All the affection he had for her had never gone away—suppressed, not erased—and now it surfaced along with the memories. Her warmth mingled with his, the feel of her skin, her hair brushing across his abdomen, her lips kissing his scars, as confident with her body as she was in her career, her sensual self-awareness that constantly enticed him, how he'd memorized the map of her freckles and the very scent of her.

Big things, little things, none he'd been able to forget.

He took her by the arm and drew her closer, bringing her body flush with his. He didn't question whether what he felt for the woman he was holding was nothing more than infatuation. Or a simple case of unrequited lust.

Without a doubt, it was more. Deeper.

Kelly was beneath his skin. In his head. In his heart.

He leaned in, lowering his face to hers slowly, giving her a chance to push him away, but she was the one who pressed closer and kissed him.

No tentative, exploratory kiss, either. It was a full, openmouthed assault he welcomed.

Rising on the balls of her feet, her arms circling his neck, she held on to him as if he were a lifeline, her fingers running through his hair as she deepened the kiss. He tightened his arms around her waist, lifting her off her feet as he devoured her mouth like a starved man.

He didn't have to worry about barricading the door this time out of fear she'd try to get away. She hungered for him as much as he did for her, and that knowledge made Hunter feel heady and turned on all at once.

She tugged him to the bed and pushed him down. Still standing, she took off her blazer, tossing it, un-buttoned her silk blouse and slipped it off, revealing a sexy bra of pale blue lace and silk that barely restrained her full breasts.

He swallowed, astonished at how they'd come full circle, back in a hotel room. "You're stunning," he said, his voice husky. Her body, her brains, her bravery—it was all stunning. She took his breath away.

She smiled. "You're pretty incredible yourself." She unzipped her pants and slid out of them. Her panties, what little of them there were, matched her bra.

His mouth went dry.

She turned around, giving him a view of her perfect heart-shaped backside as she pulled the pins from her twist. Her red hair tumbled down her back before she faced him again.

Climbing on the bed, she straddled him, leaned over and kissed him. His hands went up to hold her face to his.

Her barely clothed body rubbed against his chest and groin, making him unbelievably hard. He held her close, so tight, afraid something might ruin the moment. He slipped his fingers through her hair, so soft, so silky.

He swallowed a moan of pleasure. His straining erection wasn't a reminder of how long it had been since he'd slept with a woman—eighteen months, no one since Boston—but how much he wanted to lie between Kelly's thighs again. Needing her more now than he had a year and a half ago, he kissed her jawline, her neck, took in the scent of her luscious skin. He breathed into her ear and nipped the lobe, feeling her shiver in his arms.

"Hunter," she murmured.

While he was still capable of thinking straight, he had to ask. "What are the rules this time?"

She stared down at him, her hair falling and brushing his cheek. "None." She pressed her mouth to his in a soft kiss. "No more rules, no more boundaries between us. The only thing I need from you is honesty."

"You'll always have that. And more…"

He wanted to give her so much. He loved her like he'd never loved anyone or anything in his whole life, but before he could finish, her lips crashed down onto his. Her kisses were hungry, urgent, almost desperate.

This was everything he'd craved. The peace of mind of having her fighting at his side rather than against him. The anticipation. The desire. The love he had for her that he was finally able to feel without the burn of anger, too. Most of all hope. That's what she gave him.

Hope they'd have a future, and that, for the little while that they were in each other's arms, nothing else mattered.

Chapter Eleven

This wasn't lust.

This was affection and fire and a kind of burning need that had her shaking at her core. It wasn't like the first time they'd been together, when it had been all about fun and pleasure with no thought of consequences. This was much deeper.

She realized now that she'd been so hurt by his supposed betrayal not simply because it had been a breach of sacred trust, but also because she loved him.

Only someone she cared for so deeply could break her heart.

Despite how hard she'd tried to deny it, ignore it, resist it, she'd been in love with Hunter Wright for years. The intelligent team leader who surpassed all the others. So intense that being near him made her tingle. An indomitable will that left her in awe.

He'd forgiven her for putting him and his people in harm's way *and* he wanted her. Still.

Any reason to be scared of this connection was obliterated by his mouth on hers, his calloused fingers skimming over her body. In the middle of this hell that threatened all their lives, and with him having every justification to hate her, he made her feel like she was the center of the universe.

She didn't deserve his warmth, not after what she'd done, but she'd take it.

Grabbing the hem of his shirt, she peeled it over his head and tossed it. She ran her hands up his solid chest and over his defined shoulders, holding his gaze.

"I want you, Red."

She reached down and stroked the bulge between his legs. "I want you, too."

He stilled, his body going rigid. "That's not what I mean." He moved her hand and lowered over her, resting on his forearms. "You're so strong and resilient. You've done this for so long on your own. I don't want you to be alone anymore. Not ever again. Everybody needs someone. I want you."

He wasn't staking claim to her in some possessive way. He was opening his heart and his life to her.

She didn't know what to say, what to think. Her father had taught her to be tough, self-sufficient, to rely on no one else unless she wanted to be disappointed. Every lesson Judith had reinforced until it was ingrained in her. *Tough love*, she'd called it.

The Topaz unit had been a huge part of her life before their last mission, the closest thing she had to family besides her godmother. But there was so much of herself that she kept protected behind a wall from everyone. Price. Judith. The entire team.

Only once had she let down her guard and allowed someone else in. Hunter. In Boston.

He stroked her hair, his attention fully focused on her. It dawned on her why he had risked coming to Northern Virginia, the most dangerous place on the planet for Topaz, to see her. He'd believed she would listen to his story, watch the video of what happened at the mall and chase after the truth. Even when she'd doubted, would've sworn it wasn't possible, he'd believed.

Hunter might know her better than she knew herself.

She wasn't sure what to do with that, but she wasn't going to retreat. No more running. "I don't know how…"

He lay on his side, bringing her with him, his thigh slipping between her legs, her chest pressed to his. Sliding her arm around his waist, she held him tight, not wanting to lose *this*.

Stroking her hair, kissing her forehead and temple, he brushed his stubble against her cheek, setting off every nerve ending inside her.

She shuddered, reveling in his touch, astounded by his tenderness and patience.

"Let me be the one you turn to, you lean on." His mouth glided across her cheek and jaw, stopping where her pulse pounded in a wild rhythm. "Let me be the one you share your fears with. Let me be the one who gets past the wall." Gathering her tightly against him, he placed a searing kiss on her lips, and she nearly came undone in his arms.

She'd told him no boundaries, but he sensed her restraint. The last safeguard she still had up. He was asking her to let it go, to let him in.

Goose bumps chased tingles over her skin. He understood her in ways no one else had. Or ever would.

Pressing herself closer, she kissed him back hard and long, soaking in the heat of his body, the pounding of his heart against her chest, as desperation and desire slid into every stroke of her tongue against his.

The world outside, all the fears, faded away until the only thing that remained was Hunter. With him, she could be herself, vulnerable, flawed. This was real. Raw. Something so beautiful she'd never imagined having it in her life.

She let out a soft moan. "Yes, I want you," she said, accepting his gift of devotion and protection. Of what she hoped was his love. She was tired of doing this alone, putting her life on hold for the sake of her career. It was so hard. So lonely. He was offering her a chance at a type of happiness she'd never known, a future with a different kind of security—if they survived this. She wanted that, with him, more than anything else. "I need you." The last part slipped out without her permission.

Her father always told her that to need anyone was a sign of weakness.

Maybe Hunter was her weakness, but he was also her strength. Someone who would always have her back. Support her. Believe in her when no one else would.

Since he'd been on the run, she'd been a hot mess. On edge. At a constant nine on the Richter scale of anxiety.

But not now. Here in his arms, she was safe.

"Not a day has gone by since Boston that I haven't thought about you. Wanted you. Many times, I'll admit, with mixed emotions," he said, and she didn't doubt that on occasion he'd wanted to strangle her. "But one thing is clear to me. I need you, too." The sincerity in his voice warmed her from the inside. "All your fire and ice and everything in between."

Smiling at him, she chased down the fear slithering up the back of her throat, determined to be undaunted. Whether or not they'd have the opportunity to explore a future together was unknown. Their mutual confession, their commitment to each other was enough.

"Tell me what you want, right now," he said. "To talk about everything that you've learned? To be held? To eat? You haven't had much today. I have food for you. Just a sandwich, but it's more than you've had all day."

No one had cared for her before. Put her needs above their own.

Hunter was like no other.

She wanted all that he offered. A conversation needed to be had, probably several of them, but she was going to take this reprieve from the danger and enjoy it. He'd earned it. He'd forced her to earn it as well. She was going to take and give and remember what it felt like to share all of herself with him.

Kelly reached for his belt and undid the buckle. "I want you to make love to me first."

He caressed her face, her breast, her back, her hip, every inch of her. Everywhere he touched had her shivering with anticipation; every breath across her skin squeezed a moan from her throat. He slid a hand into her panties, and his fingers stroked her where she throbbed and ached for him.

She spread her legs, giving herself over to him, freely, happily, with no walls between them, and she was lost.

THEY'D MADE LOVE again in the shower, cleaned up and hadn't bothered to dress. He sat on the bed with his back against the headboard, watching her devour a chicken salad sandwich.

The only thing she wore was the surveillance necklace. A feat of engineering that was stylish and waterproof.

He looked over her gorgeous body, appreciating every curve, every elegant line. Her milky skin showed love bites on her neck, shoulder and thigh. He hadn't meant to mark her, but they'd gotten carried away.

Their lovemaking had been hungry, but it hadn't been frantic. Once they'd found their sensitive spots, the things they each liked and enjoyed, the things that made them both lose control, hadn't changed, they'd slid into a rhythm. The urgency building until they'd slipped over the edge, and it was as if Boston had been yesterday.

Kelly looked up from the to-go container, and her smile pierced straight through him.

He was a goner, completely caught up in the one and only Kelly Russell. At times, the memory of their one night in Boston had sometimes seemed like a fantasy he'd rebuilt in his head. Making it hotter, sexier than it had really been.

But she was more beautiful and captivating than he remembered. Her skin softer. Her mouth hungrier, sweeter. She was thinner, not eating enough, but the visceral attraction that drew him to her hadn't been diminished in the least.

Shifting closer to him, she ran her hand up his leg,

her lips pressing to his as her fingers teased the muscle and tendons of his thigh. Heat and searing need flooded him in an instant, and he was helpless to hide it.

Her grin widened. "Looks like somebody is ready for another round." She reached for the rigid proof of his arousal.

But he captured her wrist gently, stopping her. They were in a bubble of joy and desire. There was no other place he'd rather be. If he could, he'd stay in it with her forever.

Like all bubbles, it had to burst sooner or later, and they had so much to discuss.

"You have to stay away from Price until this is done," he said.

Her smile faltered and faded. "I know. I will." She pulled her hand free and wiped her mouth with a napkin. "But it's not him I'm worried about. Not directly."

It didn't take a mind reader to understand what she meant. "Quinlan."

She nodded. "Funny, Price was the one who warned me about using him. Provided Price doesn't find out that we're working together, it shouldn't be a problem."

Although as long as she was with him, she was in danger. Quinlan was out there right now trying to find Gage and the rest of them. Hunter had notified the team once he'd heard Andrew's good news about spotting Gage at the store. They were all on high alert, trying to remain invisible.

He tucked her hair behind her ear and brushed crumbs from the corner of her mouth. "I can't figure out Andrew's part in all this. Are you sure he was sent to the black site?"

"Yeah. We were together when they bagged us and transported us with hoods on. In the van and helicopter."

"How do you know he wasn't cut loose?" Maybe it had been a ruse for some reason.

"We talked along the way. Whispered, really. He was at the black site. We traveled back together, too. I'm not sure what they did to him, but he had bruises."

Hunter scrubbed a hand across his jaw. "The lie about David is what I'm hung up on. He knew he was killed from the report. Why hide it from you?"

"I've been tossing that one over, too. I don't have an answer for it."

A cell phone buzzed.

Kelly reached down over the side of the bed and picked up her pants. She yanked the phone out of her pocket and looked at the caller ID.

"Who is it?" he asked.

"Unknown number." She hit the green icon. "Hello?"

"Avocado." It was Freddie. He'd hit pay dirt, found the evidence they needed. "Get pen and paper." His voice was steady, perhaps even excited. Good signs no one had him under duress. There was background noise like he was in a car or on public transportation. He was definitely traveling.

She scrambled off the bed and went to the desk, picking up the ballpoint pen. "Go ahead."

He gave the address of a restaurant. "Twenty minutes." The line went dead.

She checked the time. "How long for us to get to Pentagon City from here?"

"About thirty-five minutes, depending on traffic."

She swore under her breath as she raced around the room, collecting her clothes. "We have to be there in twenty. Otherwise, Freddie will leave and shred everything he found."

Hunter jumped off the bed. "He didn't give us much time."

"I think that was his point." She already had her underwear on and was buttoning her blouse. "He probably wanted to keep the window small to reduce the chances that someone other than me showed up."

He shoved into his jeans. "We won't make it in twenty minutes."

"Didn't you hear what I said? We have to."

"I'm capable of a lot, but the miracle of freezing time isn't one of them." He pulled on his shirt and found his phone. The others were close enough to make it. "Who on my team would Freddie be the most amenable to talking to?"

"I don't understand how that's relevant."

He hadn't gotten a chance to tell her the others had relocated. "Who?"

Sighing, Kelly slipped on her shoes. "Probably Zee. He's met her and when I mentioned her daughter, it got to him."

Hunter dialed her number. As soon as she answered, he said, "I need a favor. It's something John won't like. I understand if you can't do it." She listened as he explained the details. "I need a yes or no."

"Yes," Zee said without hesitation.

"You have seventeen minutes. Try to get Freddie to wait. If you can't, then just get the documents."

"Got it." She hung up.

He pulled a ball cap on his head. "Zee will meet him." They grabbed their coats and hustled out the door. "She's good at winning people over."

"I'll drive," Kelly said. "The less your vehicle and plates are exposed, the better."

Good thinking. He climbed into the passenger's seat as she started the engine.

Kelly backed out of the spot, whipped the car around and hit the road. "Explain how Zee can make it to Pentagon City in time when we can't." The sharpness in her tone told him she was less than pleased with his omission.

He stifled a groan. "Bringing you to the motel compromised the location. I had to move the others. Even if they hadn't insisted, it was the smart call. I wasn't hiding it from you. We hadn't gotten around to it. There were more pressing matters to discuss."

She tightened her grip on the steering wheel, her knuckles whitening as she took the on-ramp for the interstate. "They still think I can't be trusted, after what you all put me through last night? They might not have confidence in me, but they should in that stupid drug you gave me. I'm sure you tested its efficacy beforehand."

"We did. On me." If anyone was going to be a guinea pig, it had to be him.

She shot him a concerned side-eye glance. "You must've been really desperate."

"For the truth? Yes." Besides confirming the drug worked, he needed to understand the side effects before giving it to anyone else. Including Kelly, even when he thought she had betrayed them. "John doesn't know you. He only wants to keep his family safe. You can't fault him for that. You have to admit it was possible for this to have played out a hundred different ways. Most not in our favor."

Kelly nodded. With her hair loose around her shoulders, she looked younger, innocent. Almost fragile, though she was anything but. In her head, she probably agreed with the things he'd told her, but in her heart...

"The others thought you'd help us." Hunter put a hand on her knee and squeezed. "I *knew* that you would. I didn't doubt you." Staying behind at the motel, with no backup, was proof.

"Thank you." She stared straight ahead at the road, going well over the speed limit as she changed lanes and cut around cars. "You're right. It was smart to move the others. You shouldn't tell me where they are."

What? "Kelly, you're risking your career and your life. You're entitled to know everything."

She shook her head. "No. I need to earn their trust. The way I earned yours. And we need to think worst-case scenario. The less I know, the better. Under duress, I can't give information that I don't have."

He glimpsed the sadness and hurt that tightened her features. "You would never."

"Oh, Hunter." She tapped a finger on the steering

wheel. "There's one thing I learned at the black site. Everyone, no matter how tough or stubborn, eventually breaks." She whisked a tear from the corner of her eye, but she didn't let a single one fall.

He wanted to wrap her in his arms and hold her, love her, make her forget.

Then he wanted to kill Price. For orchestrating all this. For subjecting Kelly to such pain and humiliation. That's what they did at black sites. They broke your body, your mind, your will. Bit by bit until you cracked.

She took the Pentagon City exit.

His mind was racing nonstop about the meeting with Freddie and whether Zee had made it in time. About what Kelly had endured at a black site.

But why would Price send her there when he knew she was innocent?

For appearances, to make it look good since suspicion would naturally fall on the team handler?

Or had it been for another reason?

What if it had been to keep her mind occupied on the fear and horror of the torture instead of looking for the truth?

The thought sickened him to his core. The CIA had been an anchor he had placed his entire trust in. Kelly had done the same. If Price could go to such lengths, then there was no such thing as good. The world was just a mess of gray.

Wayne Price wasn't inherently evil, but nothing else explained what had happened to his team. To Kelly.

At least, he could answer one of his questions by calling Zee. He shoved his hand into his pocket and realized he had run out of the motel so hastily he'd left without his mobile. *Stupid, stupid mistake. One for an amateur.*

"What's wrong?" Kelly asked, driving toward the restaurant.

"I forgot my cell. I can't call Zee."

"Use mine," she said, then she tensed. "No, don't. If my phone is being monitored, I don't want her cell number linked. I can't become an even bigger liability."

Precisely why he hadn't called Kelly earlier, despite how much he'd wanted to talk to her.

Not only could Zee not contact him for anything, such as an update or verification for Freddie that Kelly had sent her, but he also couldn't make sure that Zee was safe.

Out the window, Hunter glimpsed four police officers running down the sidewalk in the opposite direction, heading somewhere behind them. He turned in his seat, catching them race down the stairs of a nearby Metro station.

Hunter faced forward and glanced at the clock. They were running so late. It had taken them twenty-five minutes. The traffic had been lighter headed closer into the city as commuters were going home to the suburbs in the opposite direction, which had worked in their favor. Kelly had made great time, but not fast enough. If Zee hadn't convinced Freddie to hang around or give her the documents, they were back at square one.

"Park there." Hunter pointed to a spot. The restaurant was a block away.

"It's a tow-away zone."

"We won't be long. Two minutes. Ten at the most."

She was riveting with her fiery-red hair loose around her face, but it also made her stand out. "Do you have anything you can use to cover your hair?"

"I think I have a scarf in my purse."

Kelly was the type of woman who was prepared for anything.

She pulled into the spot and cut the engine. Taking her handbag, she rummaged around inside and whipped out a large, expensive-looking silk scarf. She wrapped it over her head and tied it under her chin. She tucked the rest of her hair that hung loose in the back of her coat.

"Perfect." He lowered the bill of his cap down. They got out of the car and hurried down the street at a trot. Glancing at his watch, he saw it was five ten. He took Kelly's hand. "Come on." They broke into a run.

He could see the restaurant about three hundred feet away on Twenty-Third Street between South Fern and South Eads. Four people were standing around outside, chatting. None of them were Freddie or Zee.

If Freddie had left in the past couple of minutes, they should be able to see him. But there was no sign of him. Hunter had interacted with him face-to-face on a couple of occasions and would've been able to spot him in a crowd.

They waited for the light to change, allowing them to cross the street. After a couple of seconds, Kelly seemed too anxious to wait any longer. A break in traffic presented itself, and she tugged him across the road at a sprint. They passed a little side alley lined with dumpsters for the various stores and eateries and headed for the entrance at a quick pace. He could see inside through the plate glass window and strained for a glimpse of Zee or Freddie.

There.

Zee sat at a table in front of the window alone. Her long spiral curls were up in a bun, and she had on a wide-brimmed, floppy wool hat. As she looked around, he caught her eye. She threw her hands up in question, as if to say Freddie had never showed. She stood, gathering her things, a laptop and some other items from the table.

The squeal of tires snatched his attention. An SUV swung onto Twenty-Third Street at a high rate of speed, tires smoking. The vehicle slowed down, the right-side window lowering.

A man wearing a ski mask stuck his head out and lifted a submachine gun.

What the hell?

Hunter stopped walking, jerking Kelly to a stop alongside him as he processed what was happening, his body tensing to react.

The guy shoved the barrel of the automatic weapon out the window. The muzzle was aimed at the four people standing in front of the restaurant. The next thing he knew, gunfire ripped loose, spraying the front of the restaurant with hot rounds. All four individuals were hit instantly, spinning and falling to the ground.

Time slowed, everything stretching out at half speed. He strategized his options from one breath to the next, but there was no way out of this. They were in trouble.

Standing in front of the plate glass window of the restaurant, they had no immediate protection in sight.

Nothing at all to stop the rounds that were about to tear into them, not even a sidewalk bistro table.

He considered hauling Kelly to the side alley behind them about forty feet away, but there was no time.

The man was still spraying bullets on full automatic, the slugs shattering the plate glass and stitching toward them like a sewing machine. The assailant's gun hand began to lose control from the vicious recoil of the weapon, giving Hunter a slim opening.

Rolling down the street at a crawl, the vehicle continued forward, only ten feet away now.

Hunter shoved Kelly down to the ground and did the only thing he could. He took the gunman head-on.

If Hunter miscalculated in the slightest, he was dead. He launched himself at the SUV. The man's eyes, framed in the balaclava, widened with shock as he spotted Hunter charging toward the gunfire. The assailant tried aiming the weapon directly at him, but Hunter beat him in the blink of an eye. Right as the bullets were about to riddle his body, he closed his hands on the hot barrel and jerked it upward.

With the man's finger locked on the trigger, the weapon cycled rounds, blasting bullets skyward, inches from Hunter's face. The guy struggled to regain control, and when the driver accelerated, the gunman almost succeeded. But the sudden change in speed allowed Hunter to wrench the submachine gun from his hands.

The vehicle hurtled down the street, the tires squealing again as it rounded a corner.

He watched as the SUV raced away, disappearing from sight, then he scanned for any other danger.

Kelly had made a beeline for the small alley that they had passed on the way to the restaurant, most likely seeking cover behind a dumpster. It was the perfect spot to seek shelter. But he found her locked in a ferocious brawl with another man wearing a balaclava who must've been waiting for a target to run there.

Hunter pulled the trigger, letting the remaining rounds in the magazine pepper the side of the building, chipping the bricks over their heads, without getting close enough to hit Kelly by accident.

The man turned tail and took off down the alley.

Hunter ran to Kelly. She was winded and the scarf had slipped down to her neck, but she didn't appear injured.

"Are you okay?" he asked, pressing a palm to her cool cheek, making sure.

She nodded. "I'm fine."

He thought about the wild spray of bullets. The plate glass window shattering. The bystanders who had been shot.

Zee.

Turning, Hunter bolted for the restaurant. Out of the four civilians who had been standing in front of the window, two were dead. A woman sat upright, holding her arm that had been shot. One man lay on his back, rolling left and right, clutching his chest. Blood stained his hands, dripping on the pavement.

Hunter's first instinct was to help him, but when he glanced inside the restaurant through the shot-out storefront, he didn't see Zee. Maybe she had been able to take cover and was staying low. He had a tough choice to make. As much as his conscience demanded he help the man, he chose his family instead. Once he knew Zee was safe, then he could help the wounded man.

He yanked open the restaurant door and rushed inside, frantically looking around.

Zee was down on the floor, the laptop beside her, blood pooling in her abdomen.

No!

Chapter Twelve

Her mind spinning, Kelly scrambled into the restaurant behind Hunter.

Everything had happened so fast. One minute she'd been focused on meeting Freddie, terrified that they'd missed him, and the next, Hunter was shoving her down to the sidewalk.

And then gunfire had ripped through the air.

Hunter dropped the submachine gun and fell to his knees beside Zee. She'd been hit. A red stain was sprouting on her abdomen.

A strangled wail came from Hunter, the awful sound reverberating through Kelly. He scooped Zee into his arms. She was alive and conscious, sucking in gulping breaths.

"I'm here. I've got you." He placed her hands over the wound. "Apply pressure. As much as you can."

Zee did as he told her and winced from the pain.

"It's going to be okay," he said. "Stay with me."

Zee. God. Kelly couldn't believe she was severely injured, bleeding out in a restaurant. She felt like she was dreaming, trapped in a terrible nightmare and couldn't wake up.

Glancing around dazedly, Kelly saw other customers down on the floor who had been shot or were still cowering under tables where they'd taken cover.

Sirens approaching split the air. The sound was growing louder with each passing second.

"We've got to go, now," Kelly said. "Come on."

Holding Zee, Hunter stood and rebalanced her weight in his arms.

"The laptop," Zee groaned. "We need it."

Kelly took off her scarf and wiped Hunter's fingerprints from the submachine gun, then she grabbed the laptop and hurried after them.

Hunter had taken off at a jog, headed back to the car. Kelly quickly caught up to them and dashed ahead. She raced into the street, holding up her palms to stop traffic and give Hunter a chance to cross with Zee.

Once they had made it to the other side, Kelly ran at a dead sprint. At the car, she opened the back door. Hunter got Zee into the car, carefully laying her down on the back seat.

"I'll drive," Hunter said, which made the most sense, since Kelly didn't know where they were going.

It wasn't as if they could take Zee to a hospital, but she needed urgent medical care.

Kelly threw the keys to him and climbed in the back, putting Zee's head on her lap. Needing to do something to help her, she reached for her go bag in the foot well. She unzipped it and rifled through the contents.

Hunter started the car and zipped into traffic, cutting off another vehicle. Several horns blared as he sped away down the street.

"Where are we going?" Kelly asked.

"To the motel, where the others are staying. Kate can help her."

Alarm streaked through her. "I can't go there." She couldn't endanger everyone else.

"We're out of options. I'm not going to pull over and just let you out on the side of the road. We don't have time to spare to drop you somewhere safe."

She considered protesting, but it would do little good. If anything, it would only add to the stress of an already dire situation.

Kelly pulled her emergency medical kit from her go bag. Controlling Zee's bleeding was the most pressing concern. She found a packet of gauze that was pre-treated with a hemostatic agent.

Before using it, she needed to see if there were multiple wounds and how bad they might be. Kelly folded back the sides of Zee's jacket. "I need to take a look."

Zee nodded and moved her hands.

Kelly lifted the hem of her sweater, peeling it up over the sticky spot where blood pooled, and gasped at what she saw.

"What is it? What's wrong?"

"She's wearing a bulletproof vest." Kelly lowered the zipper on the side of the vest, slowly, gently.

"Did the bullet hit her somewhere she wasn't covered?"

"No." Kelly tried to stop her hand from trembling. "It penetrated the vest."

"That would mean they used armor-piercing rounds."

At least the vest had slowed it down and hopefully minimized the impact. The internal damage wouldn't be nearly as bad as if she hadn't been wearing one.

Kelly pulled up the lower part of the vest to see the injury. Only one gunshot wound. She pressed the gauze with hemostatic agent on the wound and used her hand to add pressure.

"The AP rounds," Hunter said, "the man waiting in the alley. The one any trained operative would have used for cover. This wasn't random. It was planned, coordinated."

"In under twenty minutes?" She moved her hand from the wound. The gauze was soaked through with blood. She peeled it off, put on a fresh piece and applied more pressure.

"It's the only explanation," Hunter said.

"But how?"

"Price has to be monitoring your phone. He must've identified the call as Freddie's and put two and two together. Quinlan and his men must've been close enough to respond."

Kelly had hoped their precautionary measures would have been enough. She bit her bottom lip, wanting to scream in frustration. The only reason she didn't chuck her cell phones out the window was the specialized app she'd had a tech guru download on them. It constantly bounced her position between cell towers within a hundred-mile radius of her true location so no one could trace her actual whereabouts.

She'd even had an ace hacker test the app. It was air-tight, tamper-proof.

There must've been a lookout, waiting for her or Freddie to arrive.

"Did you see Freddie?" Kelly asked Zee.

"No." She groaned, her head lolling from side to side. "I was monitoring the CCTV cameras on the street from my laptop. I never saw him."

Where was he? "Maybe he got cold feet at the last minute and decided not to follow through." She hoped that was the case. The alternative was that something had happened to him.

Kelly cradled Zee's head while keeping pressure on the wound. Her tawny brown skin was ashen. Hunter needed to hurry before she went into shock.

The pretreated gauze was slowing the blood loss, but there was no way to tell what kind of internal damage she'd suffered. If an armor-piercing bullet had struck a major organ or artery.

"Hold on. We'll be there soon," Kelly said to her, even though she had no clue where the motel was located or how much longer it would take to reach it.

Zee was the glue that held Topaz together, a sister, a mother to the entire team. The one who made sure they all ate balanced meals in the field and didn't subsist off junk food. The one who gave them advice about their personal lives. She was the calming voice of reason when too much testosterone drove heads to grow hot and had mouths running even hotter.

They couldn't lose her. It would devastate all of them.

Kelly put a hand to her clammy cheek. "Hang in

there, Zee." Light glinted off something, catching Kelly's gaze. A diamond ring on Zee's left hand.

Zee was engaged to John?

The realization only added to the pressure building in her chest.

"We're here." Hunter pulled into the parking lot of a motel and stopped in front of room 151. There was a black sedan in the spot beside them.

Kelly looked around for any passersby. No one was around. In this quadrant of the motel, there were only two other vehicles. Both must've belonged to Topaz.

Hunter opened the back door, and Kelly helped him get Zee out of the car. He picked her up, and she could tell he was taking great care not to add to her discomfort. "Knock on 150," he said, hustling around the car.

Kelly pounded on the door with a fist.

The door swung open, and she faced Dean. His eyes narrowed, his body tensing as he prepared to strike.

"Zee's hurt." The words rushed from Kelly's mouth.

Dean looked past her, spotting Hunter. "Kate!" He called over his shoulder as he stepped back, letting them inside the room.

Hunter laid Zee down on the first of two queen beds closest to the door. "Tell Gage to keep a lookout," he said to Dean. "I don't think we were followed, but I can't be sure. We need to be prepared and go get John. Don't let Olivia come."

Dean gave a curt nod and took off like a shot out of the room.

Kate came out of the bathroom and froze, taking

in the scene. Then she rushed over to examine Zee. "What happened?"

"Gunshot wound," Hunter said. "AP round through her vest."

"What's AP?" Kate snatched a medical bag from the desk and pulled on latex gloves.

"Armor-piercing. It tore through the vest."

Kate's eyes widened in alarm, but she didn't slow down. She pulled out a large plastic sheet. "Help me."

Kelly hurried over to assist. They spread the plastic sheet over the second bed. Kate tossed her a bundle of sterile surgical sheets.

"You're prepared," Kelly said, unable to filter the surprise from her voice.

"I needed to be ready in case anyone got seriously injured in Venezuela."

"Laptop," Zee said through a strained breath.

"Shh." Hunter knelt beside her, took off her hat and stroked her hair. "Don't try to talk. Conserve your strength."

"There's a program. Hit control-F7 to activate it." Zee took a deep breath and winced as tears leaked from the corner of her eyes. "You'll be able to monitor the CCTV in the surrounding area. Spot suspicious vehicles or activity. See them coming."

"You're something else, you know that?" Hunter said to her.

"That's why you chose me for Topaz."

"Yeah, it is. You were the best. Even at twenty years old. You still are. We can't lose you. So, you've got to hang in there."

Hunter had handpicked each member of his team. Kelly remembered how Zee had been the one holdout. The young woman had only been with the CIA for a year, after being coerced to join or go to jail. Suffice it to say, she had legitimate issues trusting the company. But Hunter had been relentless and had eventually persuaded her to put her trust in him.

Their team had been together for over a decade. Celebrating achievements together, sharing in the pain of their difficulties, helping one another through injuries, sticking side by side no matter the adversity.

Now, one of them was critically injured.

The door flew open and a man stormed in. John Lowry.

Kelly had only seen pictures of him from his impressive service record as a Navy SEAL. His enraged presence sucked all the oxygen from the room.

John's gaze fell to Zee and then swung to Hunter, who was standing up as if preparing himself. John stalked around the bed, snatched Hunter by his jacket, swung him around and shoved him back into a wall.

The thud resonated through the room.

Dean closed the door but didn't move. Nobody else moved. Kelly was stunned, uncertain what might happen next, but it was clear that whatever it was, Hunter had no intention of defending himself.

"You were supposed to protect her!" John said, slamming Hunter against the wall a second time. "I knew this would happen. That you couldn't keep her safe!"

"I'm sorry." Hunter kept his hands at his sides. "I'm so sorry. If I could trade places with her, I would."

"But you can't. Can you?" John's hand clenched and he cocked his fist back as Kelly launched across the room to stop him.

She grabbed hold of his arm, ready to do more if necessary. She recalled from his record that he'd suffered a leg injury. If necessary, she'd exploit it. "This is my fault! If you want to hit someone, hit me."

John glanced over at her as if coming out of a murderous trance. "What in the hell are you doing here?" he said, like he was noticing her for the first time. He glared at Hunter. "Are you kidding me?"

"Honey," Zee called weakly.

John turned, looking over his shoulder. Suddenly, his hands unclenched as he let Hunter go.

Zee held out her hand to him, and he hurried to her side, sitting on the bed. He took her bloody hand in his, and his entire demeanor immediately changed. Everything about him softened as he leaned in over her.

"Oh, baby." His kissed her forehead. "What happened to you?" His voice was as gentle as cotton, but it scored Kelly's heart.

There was no doubt in her mind how much this man loved Zee, that he would move heaven and earth for her.

"It's not Hunter's fault," Zee whispered.

"It never is. Always someone else's." John looked at Kate. "Can you help her?"

"I think so." Kate was setting out equipment in a neat line along the edge of the surgical sheet. "I'm going to do my best."

"We're done with this," John said to Zee. "We're finished."

"No." She tightened her fingers around his. "The team—" she swallowed and groaned in agony "—they need us. All h-hands on deck. Numbers matter."

Topaz did need all the quality help they could get, but John was also right. Zee was injured and they had a child to think of.

"We can't be done until our names are cleared," Zee said. "Please."

"We'll discuss it later. You need medical attention."

"I'm ready," Kate said. "I need to get the bullet out, check for internal damage and stop the bleeding. Bring her over here."

Hunter stepped forward to help.

"Stay away from her," John growled. He picked Zee up and set her down on the other bed.

"Dean, I'll need your assistance," Kate said as she put on a surgical gown. "John, you can stay if you can be still and quiet."

"I will," John said.

"Kelly, Hunter, I need you two to leave," Kate said.

Hunter grabbed Zee's laptop, and Kelly followed him out of the room.

"Are you okay?" she asked, putting a hand on his chest.

"No. I won't be all right until Zee is."

She understood the sense of responsibility he carried. The weight of their lives on his shoulders. "This *is* my fault. Not yours."

He shook his head. "You were the target, but this is Price's doing."

It should have occurred to her sooner. With so much

happening so quickly, she'd barely had a chance to process everything. Price wouldn't have expected Hunter or Zee to be at the restaurant. That drive-by shooting had been meant for her.

Price wanted her dead, and since Hunter had been with her, now the man knew they were working together.

Gage seemingly materialized out of thin air and approached them. "How is she?"

"Kate's trying to help her now," Hunter said.

Gage tossed him a room key, and he caught it. "It's yours. On the corner of the second floor."

"Zee has a program set up where we can monitor the CCTV in the area. I'll activate it. Keep an eye on the footage. If you hear anything about Zee—"

"We'll let you know. How's John taking it?"

Hunter shook his head. "Not well."

"I'm surprised he didn't beat you within an inch of your life."

"I wasn't going to let that happen," Kelly said, not even if Hunter's guilt would've allowed it. They were in this together. All of them. The only way to survive was by working as a team, not beating each other up.

Gage gave her a two-finger salute. "I'll stay outside for a bit. I've got a nest on the roof with your sniper rifle."

"We'll take shifts," Hunter said. "One of us on the computer and the other on the roof. Every three hours we'll rotate."

Kelly shivered. "It's freezing out here. Wouldn't every hour be better?"

"Not from an operational standpoint," Gage said. "The fewer rotations, the less likely we are to give away the position. I've got blankets, hand warmers and a thermos of hot coffee. It'll be fine."

Hunter nodded in approval.

They were all hardened, dedicated. She'd never done fieldwork. It was best to leave it to the professionals.

Hunter took her hand and led her up the staircase to the room.

Inside, he set up the laptop on a desk and initiated the program. He sat in front of the computer with his gaze unwavering, clenching and unclenching his hands.

As she stared at his grim face that was etched with grief and worry, she couldn't deny this was reality. She detested feeling helpless and had no idea what to do. How to make this better for him. For any of them. Since they'd enlisted her to their side, they were no closer to proving that Price was behind everything.

She'd only managed to make things worse.

HUNTER WATCHED THE live video feed of six different CCTV cameras in the area while listening to the news. Kelly had put on the television once she'd stopped wearing a hole in the carpet by pacing around the room.

She made coffee and offered to take over monitoring the screens, but Hunter needed something to do.

Anything to keep his mind off how much he hated himself right now.

When he had recruited Zee all those years ago, he'd seen a beautiful, capable, strong, young hacker who was wicked smart. With the genius-level IQ to back it up. He'd also seen someone vulnerable. Someone who needed to be surrounded by people who would look out for her, take care of her. Of course, she'd wanted nothing to do with joining a team. Especially not his, where they were supposed to go into the field and eliminate high-value targets.

He'd been twenty-nine, ambitious, so self-assured that he'd lacked the foresight to consider their current predicament could ever be possible. Recruiting the best of the best for his team had been his only concern.

Then one day, she came to him with a problem. A deeply personal, painful problem. He didn't help her in a shady attempt to gain her trust. He had stepped in on her behalf because it had been the right thing to do. What she had endured at the hands of a low-life operative had made him livid. Raging mad.

But it had also been the thing that had convinced her to join Topaz.

For more than a decade, they had watched out for each other, supported one another through everything. Gage, Dean and Hunter had been like uncles to Olivia since the day she'd been born. Zee was their sister, the heart of their tribe.

They weren't a family through blood. They were a family forged by choice.

And it had been his shortsighted choice that had roped Zee into this. He could have left her alone after she'd rejected his offer the first time. She would be an analyst at Langley. Safe. Not hurt, but assured to watch her daughter grow up.

If Zee didn't pull through, he'd never forgive himself.

"Still the same hogwash," Kelly said, gesturing at the television.

During the past two and a half hours, the news coverage hadn't changed. The Arlington County Police Department was covering up the drive-by shooting, no doubt from the strict instructions of Director Price that had trickled down to their level. They were calling the incident that had killed five and wounded seven, not including Zee, *gang related*.

"What an unbelievable farce," she said, starting to pace again.

It wasn't easy being on the other side of a cover-up. He would know.

The television screen flashed a Breaking News banner and switched to a different reporter standing on a Metro station platform.

"I'm Juan Dowding reporting live from the Pentagon City Metro station, where a man was killed earlier in a tragic accident. Police have finally identified the man as Frederick Herschel."

Hunter turned to Kelly. She grew still as stone. Her chest rose and fell in shallow rhythms as she stared at the television, wide-eyed and unblinking.

"He was a dedicated, hardworking analyst at the National Security Agency in Fort Meade. Earlier today an eyewitness saw Mr. Herschel slip from the platform and fall in front of an oncoming train."

"They killed him," she said. "They killed him because I dragged him into this."

Hunter got up and went to Kelly, bringing her into his arms. First Zee and now Freddie. "We needed the documentation." They still did, desperately. "Price forced us into this position. Not you. Don't forget that."

He didn't want her beating herself up over Freddie's murder. She was under enough pressure. They were all barely keeping their heads above water. Today's events had only compounded the strain.

"Freddie didn't deserve to die," she murmured. "Especially not like that."

No, he didn't. Not any more than his team deserved to be hunted or she had deserved to be tortured by her own government that she'd selflessly served since she was twenty-one.

They'd find a way to balance the scales and get justice for everyone Price had wronged.

"I've got to get Coco," Kelly said, her voice sharpening.

"Who is that?"

"Freddie's cat. She's all alone now. I promised to take care of her if anything happened."

A ferocious mix of grief, anger and dread swelled out of nowhere and hit him hard at the mention of the cat. It wasn't about the pet who'd lost an owner. Freddie was someone's son, possibly someone's brother or uncle. There were others in his life who'd miss him. Hunter also thought about Zee. About John and Olivia. About Zee's parents. She had a strained relationship with them, but Hunter had no doubt that they loved her, their only child, with all their hearts.

He swallowed past the thickening lump in his throat. "We'll get the cat once it's safe to go to his house."

"What are we going to do about Price?" She pressed her face into the crook of his neck.

Tightening his arms around her, he sucked in a deep breath. The truth was, he wasn't sure. He was sorry that Freddie was gone, sorry they'd gotten him involved, and he was furious with Price.

But all he could think about was Zee and whether or not Kate would be able to save her life.

There was a knock at the door.

"Don't worry. We'll figure it out and get through this together." Hunter kissed Kelly's forehead and went to open the door.

Hope stood with a somber look on her pale face, her eyes pink and glassy from crying. "It's Zee," she said in a shaky voice.

Hunter's heart clenched.

Chapter Thirteen

The cold air penetrated through her clothes straight down to bone without her coat, but they'd been in too much of a hurry to bother putting them on.

Kelly rushed alongside Hunter down the metal staircase to room 150. Hope trailed behind them, dotting her eyes with a tissue. Kelly's heart pounded with fear. Every frigid intake of breath seemed to seize her lungs.

Hunter hadn't given Hope a chance to spit out what she'd come to say. He tore out of the room and Kelly stayed at his side.

They had no idea what to expect. But she braced for the worst. Prepared herself to be strong for Hunter and the rest of the team.

Hunter pushed open the cracked door, and they stepped inside the warm room.

Zee was propped up in the bed. Her eyes were open but weary and glassy, like she was still under the effects of whatever drug Kate had used on her.

Relief poured through Kelly at seeing Zee alive. She said a silent prayer of thanks, even though she wasn't the praying kind. So many lives had already been lost. She was grateful Zee was with them.

John was sitting on the left side of the bed, and Olivia, the girl who was the spitting image of Zee, sat on her mother's right side.

Kate had cleaned up any traces of the medical procedure. "I was able to stop the bleeding. She's lost a lot of blood," Kate said, "but not enough to need a transfusion. I got the bullet out in one piece. No fragments. And no major internal damage. It was a good thing she was wearing the vest and that the bullet didn't hit the aorta or puncture her stomach. She got very lucky. So did you two, from what Zee told us."

Hunter took a step toward Zee and then stopped, as though he reconsidered getting any closer to John.

Kelly put a hand on his shoulder. She understood how badly he must've wanted to hold Zee's hand, kiss her cheek, simply soak in the fact that she was alive and would be on the mend soon, but he also didn't want to intrude any further.

Behind them, Hope sniffled and blew her nose. "I was so worried about you pulling through. I'm happy to know you're going to be all right. I'm sorry I can't stop crying. Greeting card commercials have me in tears these days. My hormones are such a mess," she said, putting a hand to her stomach.

Was Hope pregnant?

Only a member of the Topaz unit would go on the run and find a way to fall in love, father a child and get engaged.

Kelly wiped the surprise from her face. "We're all relieved, Zee."

"You did good work, Kate," Hunter said. "Thank you."

Dean smiled at her and put an arm around her shoulder, bringing her in close against his side.

"No need to thank me," she said, resting her head on Dean's shoulder. "I'm only glad I was able to help."

"What I said earlier stands." John tore his gaze from Zee and looked at Hunter. "We're out."

"I understand," Hunter said. "I respect your decision."

Zee pulled John's hand to her chest, dragging his attention back to her. "I don't regret joining Topaz and following Hunter all around the world. It was the best decision I ever made. I can't even regret what happened in Afghanistan. If we hadn't been forced to go on the run and hide, I never would've met you. Other than Olivia, you're the best thing that's ever happened to me. It's because of all this that I found the love of my life."

John caressed her face with his other hand. "I love you, too, honey. You and Olivia have changed my life for the better. Saved me from self-doubt and pity. Brought me more joy than I ever thought possible. Filled up a dark place in my heart with so much light and love."

"It wouldn't have happened if I wasn't a part of this family," Zee said. "They need us, now more than ever. All hands on deck, sailor."

He lifted her hand to his mouth and kissed the back of it. "You're right. They need help, baby, but that can't be with us going forward."

Zee's eyes flared wide. She struggled to sit up in protest, her face lighting up with a fresh edge of gut-wrenching pain. John placed a steady hand on her shoulder, keeping her from moving farther. "Don't worry." His voice was soft and reassuring. "We're not abandoning them." John turned back to Hunter. "I called some friends. They'll have your back and take our place."

"You shared this situation with civilians?" Kelly asked. "Can they be trusted?"

John gave a slow, sad chuckle. "Coming from you, lady, that's pretty rich."

Taking her hand in his, Hunter captured her gaze and shook his head while giving her fingers a slight squeeze. The gesture was curt, subtle, but she recognized the meaning. He wanted her to stay out of this.

"Hold on," John said. "Are you two together?" He went to stand, but Zee gave his arm a tug and he stayed seated. "Talk about sleeping with the enemy."

"Who did you call?" Hunter asked, redirecting the conversation as he let her hand go.

"SEALs. Not civilians." John's steely gaze slid to Kelly, and she forced herself not to flinch. "Four of them on leave. One is really good with computers. He's no Zee, not even on a good day, but he's the best I could get on short notice who was willing to help with few questions asked. They're driving up from Virginia Beach and will be here before sunrise. You may be losing two of us, but you're gaining four."

"SEALs," Dean said with a hint of excitement. "Good job, man."

Hunter nodded. "You didn't have to do that. I appreciate it."

"I didn't do it for you. I did it for Zee and the others." John patted Zee's hand and stood. He crossed the room, coming closer than Kelly would've preferred. "I like you, Hunter. Respect you. There have been no issues between us until things became about this woman." He gestured to Kelly while staring at Hunter. "I have a big problem with the choices you've made recently. I have an even bigger problem with her continued involvement."

"I like you, too," Hunter said, his voice even, firm. "I think you're great for Zee and Olivia. I appreciate your perspective. More than that, I respect your honesty. You've been of tremendous value to this team. But when it comes to Kelly, you no longer have a say, because you're out. For what it's worth, she isn't the enemy." He stepped away from her and John and went to Zee, lowering to his knee beside the bed. "I didn't keep you safe. I'm sorry." Zee opened her mouth, but he continued, "It is my fault. I'm in charge. I sent you there. I put you in harm's way. John is doing the right thing by pulling you guys out. You need to recover so you can be there for Olivia."

Zee glanced at her daughter, and the young girl smiled in return.

"I won't stop," Hunter said. "Not until our names are cleared. I swear it."

John glanced at Kelly, sending a look of poison through her.

She figured it was time for her to clear the air. The

only person missing was Gage, but this felt like a now-or-never situation. "I owe all of you an apology. I've made serious mistakes and have done unconscionable things because I believed the lies that Price told me. He was very convincing. But I shouldn't have doubted any of you. I shouldn't have doubted my own judgment. I don't expect you to forgive me." She looked around the room, even at Hope, who was still teary-eyed. "But from now on I'll fight *for* you." She would fight to her last breath for them. "It's the very least that I can do."

IN THEIR ROOM on the second floor of the new motel, Hunter lay in the bed, with Kelly curled against him, and stared at the ceiling. The sun was rising. Soft morning light peeked through the curtains.

After seeing Zee would be all right, he'd relieved Gage from his post on the roof and taken over as lookout. If they had been followed, the strike team could've been waiting for the wee hours to attack when they thought everyone would be asleep. Although they had Zee's program active, monitoring the CCTV of the surrounding area, the cameras had blind spots. That's where a lookout on the roof ensured no one sneaked up on the team.

Three hours in the cold, in position in the nest, had numbed his feelings and clarified his thoughts. He finally saw a way forward.

Kelly stirred, running a hand up his chest. "Have you gotten any sleep?"

"I dozed a bit." Solid sleep had eluded him. The catnap would have to suffice.

"Do you think John's friends have gotten here?"

He hadn't heard any vehicles approach or car doors close, but they were special warfare operators who excelled at stealth. And killing.

"I'd be surprised if they haven't." He tightened his arm around her. "Do me a favor."

"Sure, anything. Name it."

"Stay out of their way," he said, and her body tensed against him. "I don't know what John has told them about you. Or me, regarding you."

"You need to mitigate any potential friction."

"Yeah." With Quinlan and his team in the mix, they needed the backup of those SEALs.

She leaned up on her forearm and stared down at him. "I shouldn't have said anything last night. I only wanted to smooth things over. As if that were possible."

He tucked her hair behind her ear and caressed her face. "You gave a good speech."

"Think so?"

"It came from the heart. Zee, Dean, Gage, they get it. I'm sure they appreciated what you had to say."

"I wonder if Hope was able to relay the message without crying."

They both chuckled, and she lay back down, putting her head on his chest. He smoothed her dark red hair away from her face and trailed his fingers in a slow stroke down her long, elegant throat and over the sexy sweep of her collarbone. Pressing his nose to her hair, he breathed in the scent of her. Cinnamon and vanilla. Spicy and sweet. She always smelled like that.

"I have an idea to get us out of this," he said.

"What?"

"I go to Price's house. Find out the motive firsthand."

Kelly shot upright in the bed and stared at him, horrified.

"Not alone." Should be easy enough to squeeze the truth out of Price, and taking the others along as an intimidation factor wouldn't hurt.

"You told me to stay away from him. I think you should follow your own advice and do the same."

"It's the only way. If you take what we currently have to the DNI, it'll seem like a reach. But if you also had a solid motive the DNI could verify through independent research, we might have a real chance."

Kelly shook her head. "We need that documentation. I can't go to the director of national intelligence half-cocked. I need concrete proof of a motive I can put on his desk. Not the word of the man we're implicating who was made to talk under duress. Can't you see how that would muddy the waters? Possibly even incline him to take Price's side in this?"

"How are we supposed to get it?"

"I'll do what I should've done in the first place." Reaching over to the nightstand, she grabbed her tote bag. She fished out her phone and dialed a number.

Who in the world was she calling?

Kelly put the phone on speaker.

The line rang and rang as Hunter sat up, wondering if anyone would answer at this hour.

On the eighth ring someone picked up. "Hello," a woman said. The voice was strong, alert, familiar.

"Hi, Judith. It's me." Hunter met Kelly's gaze as she spoke.

"Oh, my dear. I've been so worried about you since I saw the news. I went to your house last night to check on you and to take you somewhere safe, but you weren't home. I was reluctant to call. For obvious reasons."

Judith was worried about the line being monitored, as well she should be.

"I'm fine. No need to worry," Kelly said. "Can you make some time for me in your schedule today? I could still use your help."

"I won't be in the office. I'll be working remotely for the rest of the week. I felt it best to get away from it all. I wish I could help you, my dear, but that won't be possible. Do you understand *the point*?"

"I do. I understand. I'm sorry to have troubled you." Kelly hung up and grinned as though she'd gotten a completely different response from the one he'd heard.

"Why are you smiling?" he asked. "She just refused to help. Although I am surprised that you'd take the chance of asking her after what happened to Freddie."

"Judith has access to everything. She can help us, and once she does, we can keep her safe. I won't leave her side."

"But she won't help. Not that I blame her."

"I'm smiling because she just agreed to."

"Were we listening to the same responses she gave?"

"All that business about it not being possible was for Price's sake. Judith isn't going into the office, and she isn't at home. She has the same app on her phone as I do that prevents anyone from pinpointing her geolocation, but she told me exactly where to find her."

They'd been speaking in code. "And where is that?"

"The Point. It's the location where the Potomac and Shenandoah Rivers meet. Harpers Ferry."

"Her house in West Virginia?"

"Yes, but in the divorce, the house was donated to an LLC."

"Owned by Judith, I take it."

"Yes. She set it up to be able to pass her assets to her son to avoid taxes."

"Savvy woman."

"Since she's working remotely, she'll have a classified laptop with her. She can give me the documentation we need without endangering her."

Sounded lovely in theory, but things rarely worked out so simply. "She'll want to know why you need it. Once she realizes it's related to Topaz, a rogue team, one that I led, she'll refuse."

Judith never did care for him. Whenever they'd been in the same room, she'd always been brusque and cold toward him. Arctic-level deep freeze. Sometimes he wondered if that was the reason Kelly had never given a relationship between them serious consideration.

Kelly pinched her lips. "No, she won't."

"Judith will think she's protecting you by not doing it. The odds of her going against her motherly instinct toward you are slim."

"Which means it's possible," Kelly said brightly, clinging to hope, no matter how small. She jumped out of bed and padded toward the bathroom. "I'll have to turn on the daughterly charm and persuade her. Failing that, I'll beg." She blew him a kiss and disappeared into the bathroom.

He'd never thought he'd see the day when Kelly Russell would be willing to beg, much less enthusiastic to do so. When she'd told the team that she'd fight for them, she'd meant it.

Still, he doubted Judith would be persuaded. She wasn't the type who would bend to anyone else's will. A real mama bear. Judith was more likely to turn his team over to Price than she was to give Kelly any documentation that would pit her goddaughter against the head of the CIA.

The situation was a tinderbox. The wrong move a lit match.

But he knew better than to try talking her out of this. She was headstrong, tenacious, and once she set her mind to a task, there was no stopping her.

Kelly came out of the bathroom, dressed, her long red hair, vibrant as flames, up in a messy twist. She leaned over and kissed him. The surveillance necklace slipped out of her sweater, dangling between them.

With her porcelain-grained skin, high cheekbones, those cobalt blue eyes and a delicate nose, she had the most arresting face. One he wanted to look at for the rest of his life.

"Let me send someone with you," he said.

Kelly pulled away, her eyes narrowing. "You're still going to see Price, aren't you? It's the only reason you wouldn't offer to come with me yourself."

"We need to be prepared in case your way doesn't work."

"You're unbelievably stubborn."

"It takes one to know one, *Red*."

She pursed her lips with a hint of a smile. "Kicking a hornet's nest isn't a good contingency plan."

He ignored the comment. "Who are you going to take? Gage or Dean. Or both." He was worried about her and would be until they had stopped Price. There was no telling what proverbial traps the master spy had in store for them. Getting caught unawares terrified him when it came to Kelly.

"None of the above. If Judith spots anyone with me, our chance will go right out the window. She trusts me, but she'll be suspicious of anyone who tags along, especially Gage or Dean. A total stranger might make things complicated." She put on her coat and slipped the straps of her tote bag over her shoulder. "Don't under-estimate Price."

"I won't."

"Take your guys with you. The SEALs, too."

That was already his plan. "You can't resist being in charge, can you?"

They were both alphas, but this would work between them, if fate gave them a real chance. He felt it in his bones.

She grinned. "You didn't seem to mind yesterday afternoon when we were in the other motel room."

Hunter visualized Kelly straddling him and having her way. Nope, he hadn't minded one little bit. "You're quite right."

He wanted to get up, cross the room and haul her into his arms. But he forced himself not to move, knowing if he touched her, he'd kiss her sweet mouth again with its bow-shaped full lips. Then one thing would lead to another, and they didn't have time to enjoy each other.

Kelly gave him one last smile and left.

He rested his head back against the wooden frame of the bed.

Going to see Price was a big gamble. He was the director of the CIA, with his guard up. Hell, he might've even contracted bodyguards to keep him safe until this was done. The man was dangerous and powerful—and totally paranoid.

None of their options were risk-free, and this one had the potential to pay off.

But Kelly was right.

Anyone who would set them up, send Kelly to a black site and endeavor to silence his unit with a bullet would cross any line, go to any extreme to see this through to the end.

Hunter would take Gage, Dean and the SEALs, to be prepared for anything.

He knew all too well that there was no greater danger than underestimating one's opponent.

Chapter Fourteen

It had started snowing as soon as she'd gotten on the road. This was probably the last snowfall of the season. The music from the radio washed out the drone of the wipers that kept the windshield clear.

Hopefully, they'd all be alive to see spring.

Despite her worries and fears and regrets, she'd gotten the best sleep this morning. Thanks to Hunter. With him beside her in the bed, she had been able to let it all go for a little while, comforted by his presence, his warmth and the knowledge that she wasn't alone anymore. She only wished he had rested longer.

He would need his wits about him with Price.

The drive to Harpers Ferry had taken over an hour since she'd stopped at a local café that Judith loved and picked up breakfast. One thing her godmother had taught her was never to show up at someone's house empty-handed, family, friend or otherwise. Good manners aside, she'd use anything to win Judith over to her cause. Even a crustless mini rainbow quiche loaded with veggies and cheese.

She forced herself to breathe through the pressure

mounting in her chest. The last thing she wanted was to endanger Judith the way she had Freddie. This time would be different.

This time she would keep her godmother safe, she vowed to herself.

Kelly made a right, turning onto the less traveled single lane that led to the house. A white waterfall of flurries cascaded down and blanketed the road. The two-story house that sat on eight acres of paradise close to the river and tucked back in the woods came into view along with the old stable. Judith used to own horses until one day Zach had lost his love for riding.

She parked her car in the driveway alongside Judith's SUV and shouldered out of the vehicle, holding the bag from the café.

It was serene. Picturesque. Everything swathed in white, the stillness, the woods, the rush of the river not far away. The air smelled clean with a hint of pine. She'd spent more than one summer and Christmas here. The place held special memories for her, some magical and some she'd rather forget. When she was five, it was here they'd gathered around her and told her that her mother was sick, dying from cancer, and they'd explained what a godmother was. It was here that her father had died from a heart attack as she'd watched Judith perform CPR until the ambulance arrived.

It was here, in this place, she'd decided to join the CIA the way her father had always wanted.

And it was here that she needed to right her greatest sins against Topaz.

She marched up to the front walkway, determined, focused, and knocked.

A minute later, Judith opened the door and beckoned her inside out of the cold. After Kelly crossed the threshold, Judith scanned the surroundings before closing the door.

"Are you all right?" Judith wrapped her in a big hug.

"Yes, fine."

"You weren't followed, were you?"

"Of course not. I took my time. I was careful." She handed Judith the bag.

"You stopped at the Rainbow Café?"

"I figured you'd only had black coffee for breakfast."

Judith kissed her cheek. "Thank you, my dear." She gestured to the wall with a pointed finger.

Kelly hung her coat up, placing her tote bag on the hook. Then she followed the rule of the house, dropping her phone in the Faraday pouch on a shelf. It clinked against Judith's.

Faraday pouches blocked incoming and outgoing signals from smartphones, tablets and laptop computers. Judith always kept one by the front door and insisted everyone who entered her home put any smart devices inside.

"Let's get you a cup of coffee." Judith led the way to the kitchen.

Kelly sat on a stool at the expansive Carrara marble island.

Judith took a mug from the cabinet, filled it with piping-hot coffee, handed it to Kelly and refreshed her own cup. She opened the bag from the café and took a whiff. "This smells so good." She put one quiche on a plate and set it on the counter in front of Kelly with a fork.

"Aren't you having the other one?"

"I'm tempted. I wish I could, but there's so much cheese." Judith frowned. "Once you reach my age, you've got to watch your dairy intake. The inflammation can be hard on the body."

Was that her future? No carbs, no dairy. What was next? No wine, no meat?

Kelly was drawing a firm wine-and-meat line. She was not going to give up all life's pleasures.

"You eat up. You're so young, with a robust immune system. Let me live vicariously through you."

Kelly looked around, noticing Judith's laptop wasn't in the kitchen. "Do you mind if we go to your office and talk?"

"Why the office?"

Kelly shrugged and cut into the quiche with the fork. "Every important conversation I've had in this house has been in the office."

Judith sighed. "Can we save the serious talk until tomorrow? Or at the very latest until dinner? I just want to enjoy having you here, knowing that you're safe." She reached across the counter and patted Kelly's cheek. "Please. For me, let's spend the next few hours remembering what it's like to be here together. Enjoying each other's company."

She wished she could, but Hunter and the others were counting on her. Their lives had been on pause for almost year. She wasn't going to force them to wait any longer than necessary. If she could get the documents from Judith, she could be in the DNI's office before the end of the day.

"I'd like that, but there isn't time." Kelly set the fork down. "It's too important."

Judith sagged with disappointment, slumping over the counter. "I was afraid you were going to say that. You didn't come here to check on me, or because you needed somewhere safe to go. You only came because you need me to do something for you. Right?"

An acrid taste filled Kelly's mouth. She hadn't come for any of the reasons Judith had wanted. But her motives weren't selfish.

Still, her throat clenched from the burn of guilt. "I do need your help. I promise I'll come back and spend a week here with you over the summer. We'll be able to catch up properly."

"I'm not asking for a week. Our jobs are nonstop. There's always a fire to put out. I'm asking you to spend the day with me, like we used to. I've been watching the news all night about the drive-by shooting in Pentagon City. Gang-related." She tsked. "And the horrible accident with poor Freddie at a Metro station nearby. I've been worried sick about you. Life is so precious, and time goes by faster than you think. Just give me until dinner before you ask for any favors."

Shame speared through her chest. Kelly lowered her head. She didn't want to hurt her godmother. Once this was resolved, she'd make it up to her. But right now, Topaz didn't have the luxury of her wasting that kind of time. "If I could, I would, but it can't wait."

She met Judith's brown eyes. "Can we discuss this in your office?"

With a defeated look on her face, Judith nodded. "If you insist."

HUNTER HAD TAKEN his time feeling out the SEALs John had brought in to help them out. They didn't use their real names. Instead, they went by the capitals of states—Austin, Denver, Jackson, Nashville. Austin was the one who had some talent with computers.

They didn't question Hunter's authority or doubt the importance of why they were there. Brothers-in-arms, giving up their precious free time, willing to fight on John's behalf, ready to put themselves in harm's way. All because a fellow SEAL had asked them to.

Hunter was committed to getting these boys back home, breathing and in one piece.

They'd made their way to Price's house in McLean. The back of the property butted up against Scott's Run Nature Preserve, a slice of wilderness in an urban sprawl. They'd parked at the preserve and cut through it, approaching the rear of the house.

Nashville was out front on point, conducting recon. With the snowfall painting everything white and the sun climbing higher in the sky, it made subterfuge harder. It was smarter to send one man ahead to scout things out and give them the all clear rather than have one of the neighbor's dogs catch them unawareness and alert the whole block to their presence.

They all wore balaclavas and gloves so that on the

off chance they were spotted, no one would be able to identify them.

Hunter had called Price's office once they'd arrived at the preserve, to make sure he hadn't gone into the office early, though it was possible he was en route and they had missed him entirely.

Pale sunshine glinted off the snow on the ground, on the trees, on everything except the matte-black weaponry in their hands. Waiting for the cover of darkness would've been optimal, but the longer they delayed, the higher the odds of Quinlan finding them. Not to mention Hunter had no idea what kind of fallout to expect from Kelly's visit to Judith.

Staying low, they made their way through the woods. A knot of dread and uncertainty tightened in his gut. He had no idea what they were walking into. If he'd be able to rattle Price enough to get him to crack and give them the final piece of the puzzle they needed.

"You guys should come see this," Nashville said over the Bluetooth comms in their ears.

Hunter exchanged a questioning glance with Dean, who was closest to him.

They hustled through the rest of the preserve, getting to the tree line that faced the back of Price's house, and took a knee in the snow. Hunter glanced around, half expecting the house to be surrounded by armed guards, but there was no one in the immediate area.

"See what?" Hunter asked.

Nashville hand him a pair of binoculars. "The garage. Right side of the house."

Hunter peered through the lenses, focused where Nashville pointed.

Wisps of smoke wafted under the doors of the two-car garage. The hairs on the back of his neck rose on end. *What in the hell?*

Something was wrong.

He scanned the rest of the house for movement or signs of smoke or a possible fire anywhere else.

Nothing.

That knot in his gut grew bigger, tighter. "Let's check it out," Hunter said.

They burst from the tree line and swept up to the back door in formation like a coordinated unit that had worked together for a long time.

Nashville tried the knob. It turned. Unlocked. He opened the door, pushing it wide.

No alarm pinged.

If the security system had gone off, Austin had been prepared to use one of Zee's tricks to take care of it. The fact the system hadn't been armed was another bad sign.

They moved into the house soundlessly, spreading out in different directions. Silence descended around them as the sickening feeling he had ballooned inside him.

Hunter made a beeline through the kitchen to the garage. Exhaust fumes penetrated the space, prickling his senses. He reached for the knob.

Gage tapped him on the shoulder, stopping him. "Hold on." He unzipped a small backpack he'd brought with him and pulled out a couple of half face-piece respirators. As the team fixer, he was always prepared to stage a scene, make a body disappear. Ready to deal with the unexpected, including handling dangerous chemicals.

They removed their balaclavas to keep smoke from permeating the cloth and each put on a mask. Hurrying into the garage, Hunter shut the door quickly behind them.

Toxic exhaust fumes clouded the air gray. The bitter taste filled his mouth.

A Mercedes parked in the right bay, close to the door, was running. Based on the amount of smoke filling the space, he estimated the engine had been on at least a couple of hours. Maybe longer.

They drew closer to the vehicle.

"Do you see that?" Gage pointed to the tube stuffed through the cracked window into the car from the exhaust pipe.

Hunter's stomach clenched. He opened the door, letting out a noxious wave of smoke. Even with the masks, they both coughed as Hunter's eyes watered.

Wayne Price was in the front behind the wheel. His head was tipped to the side toward them. Blood and brain matter were splattered across the back of the seat. A gun lay near his right hand.

Hunter slammed the door shut, and they went back into the house.

They removed their masks and headed outside through the patio door for fresh air.

His eyes stung. His throat burned. His mind spun. Wayne Price was dead.

He handed Gage the mask and pulled the black balaclava on his face in case a neighbor was watching from behind curtains in a window.

Dean poked his head out the door. "Austin found something."

With a nod, Hunter followed Dean down a hallway to the other side of the house. They entered an office. Austin was seated behind the desk and waved them over.

Hunter came around to the side of the chair. Austin moved the mouse, and the monitor woke up, but the screen hadn't been locked.

"It wasn't password protected?" Hunter asked.

"Nope. Either that's how the man in charge of one of the most clandestine organizations in the world operates or someone had him remove it. There's also this." He gestured to a Word document on the screen that read, *I'm sorry for the pain I caused. Forgive me.*

"That's convenient," Gage said, looking at the screen from the other side of the chair.

"I think it's safe to assume we agree this wasn't a suicide, but the work of a professional," Jackson said. "My question is, who has the guts, the power and the money to have the director of the CIA killed?"

Dean pulled his mask up, uncovering his face. "Andrew Clark?"

"Let's say it was him," Gage said. "*Why* would he do it? The odds are stacked against us, not them. Honestly, he didn't need to do this. He certainly didn't need to shoot him in the head and flood the garage with exhaust fumes."

"Wow," Nashville said. "That's some serious overkill."

It bugged Hunter, because it wasn't overkill. It had been deliberate, but he couldn't figure out the point. The gunshot had done the job—the exhaust fumes would only draw unwanted attention.

"Andrew is capable of a lot. But cold-blooded murder?" Hunter shook his head. "He doesn't have the spine for it, and how does eliminating Price help get him any closer to catching us?" This came back to the *why* at the heart of this. The one question they'd been trying to answer. "We were set up to protect a surveillance program the CIA needs in order to continue operating successfully overseas," Hunter said, thinking aloud, still not certain about which one—Arcane or Silent Shadow. Both were vital, and public criticism of either would be devastating for the CIA. "A program that Price was willing to do anything to protect, including kill our team." Now Price was the one dead.

"Who else would kill to protect it?" Denver asked.

An icy chill splashed over Hunter.

No, no, no. He didn't want to think it was possible.

But only one other person had the guts, the power, the resources, the hardness, the motive to go this far.

"The head of the NSA." *Judith.* "Anything or anyone that threatens one of her surveillance programs is a threat to her professionally." And the woman he loved had just gone running straight to the real enemy. "Kelly is in danger. We've got to get to Harpers Ferry."

Chapter Fifteen

Judith sat behind her desk with her back to the windows that overlooked the snow-covered backyard. The second door in the office led to a private patio where Kelly had had countless heart-to-hearts with her godmother over the years.

"What is so pressing that couldn't wait a few hours?" Judith asked.

Kelly shifted her gaze from the classified laptop to her godmother. "I still need the documents that Freddie found for me."

"Freddie's death wasn't an accident, was it?"

"I don't think so."

"Were you somehow involved in the drive-by shooting?"

"I was the target."

Judith squeezed her eyes shut, clutching the arm of her chair as though she'd gotten dizzy for a moment. Then she looked at Kelly. "What is this about? And why is Price on the warpath?"

Kelly cleared her throat. "I need to know the truth about Ashref Saleh and why he was really killed."

Judith straightened in her chair with that laser-focused, command-the-room way she had about her. All vestiges of a loving godmother vanished in a blink. "Ashref Saleh? Is all this about the rogue Topaz unit?"

Sweat rolled down Kelly's spine. "Yes. It is."

"I'm confused." Her eyes narrowed as her tone turned cold and hard. "I was under the impression you already knew why and were in the process of hunting down those traitors."

"It turns out things are more complicated than I was led to believe." Less was always more when it came to Judith, but she didn't see a way around telling her the whole story.

Her godmother's jaw clenched, her gaze raking over Kelly with a look that could strip the paint off the walls. "I don't think it's complicated at all. I think it's about one man. Hunter Wright."

"No." Kelly scooted to the edge of her chair and leaned forward. "This concerns the entire team."

"Have you seen him?" When Kelly didn't immediately respond, Judith continued, "You better tell me you have more common sense than to let that man get into your head, filling it with garbage, ridiculous theories that'll ruin your career."

Kelly's stomach rolled as she replayed the things Hunter had said in the motel room about how this conversation would go. "I haven't seen him. I've done some digging into—"

"Now you're lying to me?" Judith shook her head. "You have a love bite on your neck, and the smell of a man is all over you. Did you even bother to shower after you crawled out of his bed and came rushing to me to help him, an enemy of the state?"

Shame and guilt bubbled up in her throat, choking her. Before she could gather her thoughts for a worthy response, a car door slammed closed outside.

They both looked toward the hall.

"Who's here?" Kelly asked.

"It must be Zach. He was the one who suggested I come up here to avoid the news frenzy that would be outside Fort Meade this morning because of Freddie Herschel. We have to draft a statement to release to the media." She leaned back in her chair. "He was also the one who told me you were only coming here to get something out of me." A hint of pain flashed across her face. A second later, she'd wiped her expression clean.

"You told him I was coming?" *Why would she do that?*

"He predicted it last night, and I confirmed it this morning. You show up at my office, wanting to tap an analyst because you've been locked out of certain files at Langley. Then one of my senior guys turns up dead. Zach put two and two together. He figured you didn't get what you needed and would have no qualms endangering me in whatever you've gotten yourself involved in. Apparently, that's Hunter Wright."

The front door opened. A cold draft blew through the house, reaching the office. Footsteps came down the hall.

Kelly turned, glancing over her shoulder as Zach appeared in the doorway.

"You were right," Judith said to him. "She doesn't

care about me. The only thing she's concerned about is Hunter. Can you believe she wants me to help a traitor to this country, a fugitive on the most-wanted list of every law enforcement agency and Interpol?"

"I can believe it." Zach strode into the room, up to his mother, and put a hand on her shoulder. "Did you give any thought to how this could hurt her?" he asked Kelly. "What the possible impact would be to her career?"

She stared at her godmother. "I don't want to put you in this impossible position." If there were another way, a better way…

"Then don't." Judith's voice softened along with the look in her eyes. "Think about my life and your own. You already got Freddie killed. How many more need to die?"

"I'm here trying to prevent that. I'm trying to save lives. Those of the Topaz unit. They were set up to assassinate Ashref, and I won't stop until I prove it. With proof of a motive, I can take the rest of the evidence we have and go to the director of national intelligence. Make sure that Price pays for what he did. I'm begging you to help me. I promise I'll keep you safe. Topaz will protect you."

Judith scowled at her, a look she knew too well, telegraphing disappointment. "Oh, my dear, I'm not the one who needs protection. I've been the one protecting you."

Kelly recoiled in her chair, not understanding what she was talking about.

"Ashref Saleh found out about Arcane," Judith said slowly, but the words plowed into Kelly like a high-speed train. "We intercepted a conversation of his where he was planning to hold a press conference to tell the world about how we spy on our allies, which wouldn't have been too detrimental by itself, but somehow, he'd learned about our methods and how to circumvent them. Now that would've been damaging."

That was the understatement of a century. It would've sent shock waves through the intelligence community, crippled CIA operations abroad and ended Judith's career.

It was the kind of thing you had buried by any means necessary before it buried you.

"When I approached Wayne Price about a solution to our mutual problem, he was unwilling to cooperate with my proposed methods, which left me one option. Blackmail. I had unsavory information about him. Something he never wanted disclosed to the public. Once he was on board with my plan to have Ashref assassinated, I chose Topaz for the mission."

The declaration unhinged Kelly's jaw. She shook her head, not wanting to believe her godmother was capable of this. "Wh-what? Why them?" Not that any team should have been set up and painted as traitors, but this felt deeply personal. A direct attack against her.

"Because your relationship with Hunter Wright needed to end," Zach said.

"He was a distraction," Judith said. "An impediment to you reaching your full potential. I even had my private IT expert create the video of Hunter outside the bank in the Cayman Islands. He altered real footage of him in Miami. From what Wayne told me, after you watched the clip, it sealed the deal. You believed the story hook, line and sinker."

It was true. Kelly had swallowed the lie they'd spoon-fed her and had presumed them guilty. "You had no right. To meddle in my life. To destroy theirs."

"I was doing you a favor," Judith said, anger festering just beneath the surface.

Kelly sat stunned and reeling, trying to wrap her mind around what this meant. "The black site, where I was taken? Were you behind that, too?"

"Of course. I knew you wouldn't let this go. Not unless I gave you something else to focus on. Like your own survival."

Something inside Kelly withered. "So you had me and Andrew tortured?"

Judith made an amused sound, almost a snort. "You still haven't put it together?" She cackled. "Andrew works for me. He's my inside man who was keeping an eye on Wayne and you. For the record, he was never interrogated."

"But he had bruises. I saw them."

"He was roughed up a little to make it convincing. To sell you the idea that you two were in it together. But he was the one who oversaw your torture."

The more Judith confessed, the more a sickening anxiety churned inside Kelly. The last bit of hope for a misunderstanding died. This was the demon she'd been battling for almost a year. Her godmother. "How could you do that to me? How could you let him… Andrew…" Her heart crumbled. The pain swamping her was so intense, so brutal, it stole her voice. There were no words for this. The magnitude of such a betrayal was unfathomable.

Unconscionable.

"In addition to more money, it was a nonnegotiable for him. I had your predecessor eliminated in the 'avalanche,'" she said, using air quotes, "to clear the way for you to be promoted over Andrew. How could I not give him the one thing he asked for?"

Horrified, she stared at the woman who had helped raise her. The same one who she always thought of as too perfect to measure up to her example. Of how to be a woman. A leader. A mother. "Do you have any idea how I suffered? The nightmares I still have about that place. The anxiety. The paranoia. The psychological scars it left. How dare you?" The words left her mouth like a barrage of bullets.

"It was for your own good. Temporary trauma to keep you from digging where your nose didn't belong. And it worked, too. Better than I expected." Judith sounded so pleased with herself, so smug. "It had you chomping at the bit to tear Topaz to pieces. Then Hunter Wright got to you and set this whole disaster in motion. I warned Wayne to keep you focused and from stirring up any trouble. Since he couldn't even do that right and had the nerve to let Andrew run the op that almost got you killed in Pentagon City, I had him taken care of earlier this morning. *For you.*"

The last two words seared through her.

One heartrending blow after another. She couldn't take much more. "Price? He's dead?"

"I had the whole thing worked out once I realized

Zach was right and that you'd come to me again for help. If you had only waited until dinner, not even that long. I made sure Wayne's body will be found soon, if it hasn't already. A neighbor walking their dog will see smoke coming from his garage and report it. Then I was going to convince you that Hunter was responsible. The police will find his fingerprints on the scene."

Hunter.

Thinking of how Judith had manipulated this tragedy into something even more devastating sent an ache through every cell of her body. Hunter and his team had been set up because of Kelly's attachment to them. Her love for them. For Hunter.

"The situation would've been resolved," Judith said, "with you back on the right side of things. On my side. But you had to go and ruin it. By sleeping with him."

"What?" Zach said, his gaze bouncing between them.

"Yes." His mother patted his hand. "She's been with him instead of recognizing the perfect partner she could have in you. It's the reason she's hell-bent on helping that man."

Rage burst through Kelly like a strip of firecrackers exploding. "You're going pay for this. For all of it. You're going to rot in prison."

"No, I don't think I will." Judith slipped her hand in her pocket and held up a fob. A sad smile tightened across her mouth as she hit the button. "I'm sorry about this. After your father tried to stand in the way of my appointment to director of the NSA because he thought I was unfit, unstable, I poisoned him, but I promised myself I would look after you," she said, and bile rushed up Kelly's throat, making her want to heave. "Ensure you got to the very top of the CIA and that nothing would stand in your way. Unfortunately, now it comes to this."

Zach's gaze lifted to something behind Kelly.

In the reflection of the window, she caught a glimpse of a man. Six-two. Muscular. Bald.

Quinlan.

Fear crystallized her blood.

A flash of wire swept past her face. Without thinking, she reacted, thrusting a hand up. Her wrist caught the garrote meant for her throat. The wire of the strangulation device bit into her skin, locking her arm in front of her neck. She flailed, trying to break free.

"Mother! What are you doing?" Zach lunged to help her.

Judith snatched his arm and dragged him backward. "What does it look like I'm doing?"

Kelly's heart thudded against her rib cage as she struggled to get loose from Quinlan's vicious hold. The wire dug savagely into her wrist, breaking the skin, drawing blood as the pressure on her arm lodged against her windpipe and cut off her oxygen.

If she lost consciousness, it was game over.

She slammed her foot up onto the edge of the desk and pushed with all her might as she thrust her body back, sending the chair flying down to the floor.

The swift change in angle forced Quinlan to adjust and lower himself in response, but he didn't let go.

She threw her other foot up and back, kicking him in the head. Once. Twice.

His hands opened, dropping the garrote as he instinctively clutched his face. She flung the wire away, rolled onto all fours and spun with her leg extended, plowing a boot heel into his knee.

An *oof* left his mouth, but he didn't fall as she had hoped.

Kelly scrambled backward and climbed to her feet. A quick glance over her shoulder at the door that led to the patio told her there was no escape. Another man from Beta team was standing outside. She was trapped.

Breath tight in her lungs, her heart a jackhammer, nerves jangled, she welcomed the adrenaline flooding her body. She'd need every drop of it.

Zach yanked loose of his mother's grasp. "You're not supposed to kill her! She's mine! You promised."

Judith slapped him hard across the face, the sharp sound bouncing off the walls. "Pull yourself together. Remember who you are. A Farren! We don't fall to pieces." She turned to someone else entering the room. "Get him out of here."

Two more men from Beta team entered. One grabbed Zach and hauled him out. The other came up alongside Quinlan, helping him block the other door.

"Don't kill her just yet," Judith said. "First, we need to find out where Topaz is so you can finally take care of them once and for all. Then you can dispose of her." Judith's gaze slid to Kelly. "You could've had everything. Led the CIA. Had Zach for a husband. Me, not only as an ally in the intelligence community, but as your mother-in-law, too. If only you'd heeded the warnings. If only you had been loyal, to me." She spat the words through gritted teeth. "Now instead of punishing Andrew and this beast," she said, waving a hand at Quinlan, "for targeting you, Andrew will get to wear the crown." With a heavy sigh and a distressed shake of her head, Judith strode out of the room.

Quinlan smiled, his teeth bloody from her blows to his face. "I bet you're wishing I had tossed Andrew Clark out of that helicopter now, aren't you?"

"As a matter of fact, I am." Widening her stance and raising her fists, she braced herself for what was to come.

AFTER RUNNING THROUGH the woods alone, Hunter came to a sliding stop and took up a position, lying prone, concealed by trees in the rear of Judith's house. Out of the group, they'd agreed he was most likely the best shot at a distance. The others were surrounding the house, preparing to breach.

A ball of dread had lodged in his chest as they'd sped to Harpers Ferry. Now his heart was racing, and he was anxious to find Kelly. To get her out of the house. The place was crawling with mercenaries. There had been additional vehicles parked on the far side of the old stable, hidden out of sight.

Looking through the scope of his sniper rifle, he spotted a man posted outside a patio door.

Past him in the office, Hunter saw Kelly. She was in a chair with her arms behind her back at an awkward angle, and it seemed her wrists were bound. Her bottom lip was bloody. Her hair was disheveled. The office was a wreck, as if there'd been a knock-down, drag-out fight. His heart squeezed like a fist at the thought of what she must've been through.

Quinlan stood in front of her, his mouth moving—he was talking to her.

Kelly shook her head, saying something in response.

Quinlan slapped her backhanded, so hard that her head twisted, and she nearly fell from the chair, but before she could, he grabbed her chin and wrenched her up in the seat.

A surge of rage rushed through Hunter, faster and hotter than anything he'd ever known. He wanted to kill that man. Storm inside the house and do it with his bare hands. But to help Kelly get out of this alive, he had to remain calm and calculated.

He sighted back through the scope and waited for his team to make their move. Opening fire now on Quinlan or the guy standing outside would be premature. He didn't have a full view of the office. Another man, armed, could be standing in a corner or near the doorway out of his line of sight.

Quinlan drew close to Kelly. The bastard smiled, laughed in her face.

She threw a forward headbutt into the man's skull.

He staggered backward, only a step or two, blood gushing from his nose. As he wiped at it with his hand, anger radiated from him in waves. His face twisted into a dark scowl. Raising a fist, he punched her in the stomach.

Hunter's whole body clenched.

Kelly doubled over, coughing and trembling as though she'd felt the blow down to the bone. Quinlan yelled at her. Then he reached behind her back and did something that made Kelly rear back and scream in agony.

What was he doing to her?

Had he broken her hand and was applying pressure to a fracture?

Whatever he did to her, the pain had been instantaneous and horrific.

Fury spiked through Hunter, kicking up a revving sensation in his chest. Gritting his teeth, he caressed the trigger. An inner voice cautioned him to wait, to remain steadfast, but he couldn't stand by and watch Kelly get beaten. He wasn't equipped to do it.

He tapped the comms in his ear. "You need to hurry up before I do something rash."

"Hold position," Nashville whispered in a detached tone. "Preparing to enter on my count."

Hang on, Red. We're coming for you.

Hunter took comfort in the sound of the countdown in his ear.

"Three," Nashville said. "Two. One. Breach!"

The din of percussive bangs, thuds, shouts and gunfire erupted in rapid succession, blending in a blur.

SEALs were experts at combat in close quarters. Hunter was relying on their experience, combined with the skill sets of Gage and Dean, to squash the other mercs and drive Quinlan out through the back door into the open.

As the others took out targets and cleared the house, Hunter held his position, peering through his scope. Finger on the trigger. Ready to pull it.

The man posted outside the door had drawn his weapon, his head on a swivel looking for incoming targets. As Hunter had suspected, a third man emerged from a corner in the office that had been beyond his line of sight and hustled toward the inner door, heading for the hall.

Now. This was his chance.

But before he could get Quinlan in his crosshairs, the man grabbed Kelly by the hair and yanked her up onto her feet.

Come to me. Don't go deeper into the house. Come to me. Hunter repeated the words, over and over.

A prayer.

A mantra.

A war cry.

Quinlan held a gun to Kelly's head and locked his free arm around her neck, pulling her back against him. He steered her toward the patio door.

That's it. Keep coming.

The second man scanned the perimeter, providing cover for Quinlan. Gunfire continued inside the house along with the thunderous sound of flash-bang grenades designed to stun and temporarily disable a person's senses.

Quinlan shoved his way outside, using Kelly as a human shield. Her hands were restrained behind her, but her feet were unbound. He shuffled her forward, keeping his head behind hers like he was prepared for a sniper.

The second guy changed position, moving to cover

Quinlan's back in case anyone came through the house and attacked them from behind.

With the gun to Kelly's head, Hunter was reluctant the pull the trigger. But he couldn't let them get around the side of the house to a vehicle. He had to take action before that happened.

He thought about what to do as he weighed his options. They were limited. He was too far away to rush either man and hope for the best.

Taking out the second man first might work, since he was positioned behind them, closer to the door.

Quinlan would have to turn around to see what happened to him, leaving his back exposed for Hunter to take a shot.

Hunter adjusted the side knob for windage and put the other guy in his crosshairs. He took a breath, his finger on the trigger. On the exhale, he squeezed. The attached silencer swallowed the sound, and the man dropped.

Quinlan must've heard the body fall, because he froze. But he didn't turn around as Hunter had needed him to. Instead, Quinlan kept the muzzle of the gun pressed to Kelly's temple with her still trapped in front of him and stared at the tree line, searching for the shooter.

For Hunter.

What he feared by holding the position was that one of his men would make it to the office and that Quinlan would panic. Possibly shoot Kelly.

"Come out!" Quinlan said. "Or she's as good as dead!"

Hunter removed the safety from the nine-millimeter

with attached sound suppressor that he had in his shoulder holster under his jacket. "Okay. Just don't hurt her." He got up from his position, exposing himself. With both hands raised, holding the rifle out in the air, he stepped out from between the trees.

Quinlan tightened his hold on her. "Drop the rifle."

Still walking forward, Hunter kept drawing closer to them. "Let her go first."

"This isn't a negotiation. Drop it or I'll kill her right now," Quinlan ordered.

The fear on Kelly's face was palpable, but he knew that it was more for him than herself. She shook her head as her busted bottom lip began to tremble. "Don't. He'll kill us both."

"Shut up!" Quinlan jerked back the arm locked around her throat, choking her.

Hunter took another step and another. "All right. Please, don't hurt her anymore."

There was desperation in Quinlan's cruel eyes, and that made him even more dangerous. Because he'd do absolutely anything to get out of this and save his own skin.

"Stop where you are," Quinlan demanded, jabbing the muzzle of his gun into her temple so hard that she winced. "Not another step."

Hunter's throat went bone-dry. "No one else needs to die." He slowly lowered the rifle to the ground, but he was still too far to lunge for the man. A few more feet and it would've been possible.

Now there was nothing stopping Quinlan from shooting him.

He was counting on the merc to seize the opportunity. Hunter was ready, but he'd have to move fast the second Quinlan pulled the gun away from Kelly's head. The probability was high Hunter would be shot, but it was a risk worth taking if it meant he could save Kelly.

Quinlan moved the muzzle, swinging the gun in his direction as Hunter drew the nine-millimeter from his holster.

Kelly rammed her elbow back into Quinlan's ribs, throwing off his aim. Giving Hunter the clean shot he needed.

He pulled the trigger twice. Bullets whispered through the air, putting Quinlan down with two in his chest.

A flash of movement registered in the patio door. Judith. She was holding a gun, pointed at Kelly.

His heart seized. Hunter whirled and raised his weapon. Too late.

A gunshot rent the air, sounding like an explosion.

Kelly spun and fell to the ground. The snow was splattered red with her blood.

Hunter was about to fire at the woman responsible for this entire mess, sending Judith straight to hell where she belonged, when Gage charged out of the patio door, tackling the older woman to the cold earth.

Instantly, Hunter was moving.

"Kelly!" he cried as he ran to her. His legs weren't moving fast enough, as though he was treading through quicksand.

She was facedown.

Dropping to his knees, he pulled a butterfly knife

from his pocket and cut the zip tie binding her. He noticed the deep gash on her wrist but was frantic with worry, terrified she'd been badly injured, and turned her over onto her back.

She blinked up at him. *Alive.* She was alive. The snow around her was red, blood splattered across her sweater. He couldn't be sure where she'd been shot.

"Hunter." Face bruised, she clutched her left arm and sat up, groaning.

The bullet had hit her in the shoulder.

He sat on the ground and gently tugged her into his chest. A flood of relief nearly brought tears to his eyes. Gratitude clogged his throat. "You're going to be all right."

She rested her head against him. "I can't believe you're here."

Stroking her hair, he kissed her forehead, her cheek. She was alive, safe and in his arms, and he was never letting her go.

Kelly turned her head toward Judith, who had been restrained and was being hauled up off the ground by Gage.

"Why couldn't you be loyal?" Judith screamed at her. "Why! After everything I've done for you. Ungrateful. Selfish. Brat."

Gage dragged the raving woman into the house.

"Oh, no," Kelly muttered.

"What's wrong?" He looked her over once more to be sure he hadn't missed an injury. "What is it?"

"Judith killed Price and planted your fingerprints at his house for the authorities to find. It'll be her word and Zach's against ours. She'll twist and manipulate everything." Kelly looked at him, her eyes glassy, exhaustion stamped all over her. "The police may not believe us about what happened. I can't lose you. Not again."

"It's going to be okay, Red." He smiled. "We've got Judith's confession recorded."

"But how?"

He took the pendant of the necklace between his fingers and held it up. "As soon as you left the motel alone, I activated it because I was worried about you. I left the computer with Hope and Kate. Asked them to watch out for you and if you ran into any trouble to call me. Sure enough, they did, but we were already on the way here."

"You knew? About Judith?"

"I suspected after we found Price dead at his house."

Pressing her mouth to his, she gave him a tender kiss and hissed in pain at the pressure to the cut on her lip.

"I'm sorry I didn't get here sooner," he said, staring at her bruises, hating that she'd been hurt.

She leaned against him. "Thank you."

He put his arm around her. "For what?"

"For being you. For following your instincts. For coming here for me."

He smiled, even though she couldn't see it. "I'll always be here for you. You can count on that."

Epilogue

Four months later

The sun was low on the horizon over the water of Jamaica Bay, painting the sky dusky orange and purple. With her arms entwined around Hunter's neck, Kelly stared in his crystal-blue eyes, swaying with him on the dance floor of the Bay Resort on Breezy Point in New York.

"The wedding was so beautiful," she said. "Zee is such a gorgeous bride." She glanced over at the couple, who were also dancing.

The bride wore a formfitting gown of champagne silk with a deep V neckline that was sexy yet tasteful. The fabric artfully gathered in all the right places to ensure flattering lines all over her body. Her long hair was in a chic updo with loose spiral curls framing her face.

John wore an impeccable tux. Classic. Debonair.

They'd gotten married at sunset on the beach outside the Bay Resort.

"One of the sweetest parts of the ceremony," Hunter

said, "was when John gave Olivia a ring, too, and vowed to be the best father that he could."

Kelly had gotten choked up by it. The heartfelt declaration had even made Zee's parents teary-eyed. "This has been a perfect day." She felt lucky to be a part of it.

She glanced around the reception hall. It was packed with SEALs from John's side, cops from Zee's and operatives who were thrilled to see them tie the knot. Only at a Topaz unit wedding.

Judith was behind bars, awaiting a trial that would never be held in the public eye. Andrew was also locked up, but he had copped a plea deal and provided a sworn statement against Judith. Zach had been fired from the NSA. No charges had been brought against him due to the lack of incriminating evidence.

The Topaz unit had been exonerated, fully cleared of any wrongdoing and reinstated to the CIA with commendations for meritorious service and back pay for the time they had spent on the run, trying to clear their names.

Kelly was allowed to keep the position of deputy director, and the president had appointed a new director of the agency. Only Hunter had resigned, choosing to take a job as a contractor, working for a private security firm to prevent any future conflicts of interest.

Things were as they should be.

Gage sat beside Hope with a hand on her growing belly. They'd made plans to get married right after the baby was born.

Dean, his brother, Lucas, and Kate toasted to something with bubbly. The trio talked and laughed, inseparable. It warmed Kelly's heart to see the two brothers patch things up and have a fresh start together after everything they'd been through.

"Have I told you how spectacular you look?" Hunter twirled her around, letting her spin in the sapphire dress that matched her eyes, and brought her back flush against his solid body.

"Yes, you have, but feel free to do so again."

They both chuckled.

"Having you in my arms, living together, I feel like I won the lottery."

"I'm definitely the winner. You cook. You change Coco's litter box. You're great in bed and easy on the eyes," she said, and he patted her backside. "Easy, tiger. Don't start something you can't finish." More laughter flowed between them. "Seriously, I am the winner. I learned very early on not to show anybody who I really am because I thought nobody would see me and love me for it. That I wouldn't be good enough. But then you made me feel like I was everything you ever wanted."

"You are." Sincerity gleamed in his eyes.

"Your heart is so strong, and your belief in me surprises me every day. You taught me how to feel safe in a world where tomorrow isn't guaranteed. You showed me what a family is supposed to be. I don't ever want to be without you. I love you so much."

"I love you, too." He cupped her face in his hands and kissed her. "You just stole my thunder."

"What do you mean?"

"I was going take you outside, pull out the diamond

ring I have in my pocket and propose, but I don't think I can top that."

Her heart fluttered in her throat, and she tensed. "You were?"

"I was." A devastating grin spread across his lips. "I guess I'll have to keep the ring."

"I don't need a ring." Slipping her arms around his neck, she pulled him close. "All I'll ever need is you."

He kissed her again, running his hand up and down her back, making her entire body tingle. "So does that mean I can return it and get a refund?" He raised an eyebrow.

"No, I'll still take the diamond."

He laughed, and she grinned up at him as her heart swelled to overflowing.

A perfect day indeed.

* * * * *

**WE HOPE YOU ENJOYED
THIS BOOK FROM**

⊕ HARLEQUIN

INTRIGUE

Seek thrills. Solve crimes. Justice served.

Dive into action-packed stories that will keep you
on the edge of your seat. Solve the crime
and deliver justice at all costs.

6 NEW BOOKS AVAILABLE EVERY MONTH!

#2055 CONARD COUNTY: MISTAKEN IDENTITY
Conard County: The Next Generation • by Rachel Lee

In town to look after her teenage niece, Jasmine Nelson is constantly mistaken for her twin sister, Lily. When threatening letters arrive on Lily's doorstep, ex-soldier and neighbor Adam Ryder immediately steps in to protect Jazz. But will their fragile trust and deepest fears give the stalker a devastating advantage—one impossible to survive?

#2056 HELD HOSTAGE AT WHISKEY GULCH
The Outriders Series • by Elle James

To discover what real life is about, former Delta Force soldier Joseph "Irish" Monahan left the army and didn't plan to need his military skills ever again. But when a masked stalker attempts to murder Tessa Bolton, Irish is assigned as her bodyguard and won't abandon his mission to catch the killer *and* keep Tessa alive.

#2057 SERIAL SLAYER COLD CASE
A Tennessee Cold Case Story • by Lena Diaz

Still haunted by the serial killer she couldn't catch, police detective Bree Clark doesn't hesitate to accept PI Ryland Beck's offer of redemption. The Smoky Mountain Slayer cold case has gone hot again and working together could bring the murderer to justice. But is the culprit the original slayer—or a dangerous copycat?

#2058 MISSING AT FULL MOON MINE
Eagle Mountain: Search for Suspects • by Cindi Myers

Deputy Wes Landry knows he shouldn't get emotionally involved with his assignments. But a missing person case draws him to Rebecca Whitlow. Desperate to find her nephew, she's worried the rock climber has gotten lost...or worse. Something dangerous is happening at Full Moon Mine—and they're about to get caught in the thick of it.

#2059 DEAD GIVEAWAY
Defenders of Battle Mountain • by Nichole Severn

Deputy Easton Ford left Battle Mountain—and the woman who broke his heart—behind for good. Now his ex-fiancée, District Attorney Genevieve Alexander, is targeted by a killer, and he's the only man she trusts to protect her. But will his past secrets get them both killed?

#2060 MUSTANG CREEK MANHUNT
by Janice Kay Johnson

When his ex, Melinda McIntosh, is targeted by a paroled criminal, Sheriff Boyd Chaney refuses to let the stubborn officer be next on the murderer's revenge list. Officers and their loved ones are being murdered and the danger is closing in. But will their resurrected partnership be enough to keep them safe?

Chapter One

Maintaining a white-knuckle grip on the steering wheel while
negotiating the treacherous curves up Prescott Mountain on his
daily commute was typical for Ryland Beck. *Smiling* while he
resolutely refused to look toward the steep drop on the other
side of the road *wasn't* typical. Nothing, not even his phobia
of heights, could dampen his enthusiasm this chilly October
morning. Today he'd begin his investigation into a serial killer
case that had gone cold over four years ago.

Bringing down the Smoky Mountain Slayer was the challenge
of a lifetime. No suspects. No DNA. No viable behavioral
profile. In spite of the lack of evidence, Ryland was determined
to put the killer behind bars. He wanted to give the families of
the five victims the answers and justice they deserved.

Unfortunately, what he couldn't give them was closure.
Closure, as he well knew, was a fictional construct. The death of

a loved one would always leave a gaping hole in the hearts and lives of those left behind. But knowing the victim's murderer had been caught and punished would go a long way toward making the excruciating grief more bearable.

He continued winding his way up the mountain toward UB headquarters as he considered the limited information he'd found on the internet about the killings. The Slayer's modus operandi was consistent: all of his victims were strangled, their bodies dumped in the woods in Monroe County. But aside from them being young women, the victimology was all over the place. Their educational and economic backgrounds varied, as did their ethnicity. Some were married, some weren't. Some had children, some didn't. All of that made it nearly impossible to build a useful profile to help figure out who'd murdered them.

The detectives from the Monroe County Sheriff's Office had deemed the case unsolvable. But here in Gatlinburg, Ryland had a unique advantage: an über-wealthy boss who knew firsthand the suffering a victim's family endured when a murder case went cold.

Seven years after his wife was killed and his infant daughter went missing, Grayson Prescott had given up on the stagnant police investigation. He decided to create a cold case company called Unfinished Business. Just a few months later, UB had solved the case. Now, the thirty-three counties of the East Tennessee region had formed a partnership with UB and were clamoring for them to work their cold cases.

Don't miss
Serial Slayer Cold Case *by Lena Diaz,*
available March 2022 wherever
Harlequin books and ebooks are sold.

Harlequin.com